Space Truckers

A Novel

by

Jim Mortimore

based on the screenplay by Ted Mann

B⬛XTREE

First published 1996 by Boxtree
an imprint of Macmillan Publishers Ltd
25 Eccleston Place, London, SW1W 9NF
and Basingstoke

Associated companies throughout the world

ISBN: 0 7522 2218 X

135798642

A CIP catalogue entry for this book is available from
the British Library

Typeset by SX Composing DTP, Rayleigh, Essex
Printed and bound in Great Britain by
Mackays of Chatham plc, Kent

For
Andrew Dymond
A perfect example of how it shouldn't be done –
And how you can paper over the cracks if it is

Contents

Contents

Deniable

Here's the deal:

I could tell you that Triton is of such and such a diameter, of so and so a mass and with such and such an atmosphere. I could tell you it wobbles messily round a big blue planet called Neptune and that, from orbit at least, and in the right light (i.e., total eclipse) it looks sorta cute.

Point of fact, all you really need to know about Triton is that it's an A-1, prime grade, shitheap ball of ice, with ground like a frozen fart and air that'd rot even your ma's best frying pan; whose only good point, at least as far as any respectable real estate in the solar system is concerned anyway, is that it is several long steps past the ass end of beyond.

Which is just peachy as far as the Company is concerned. The Company loves it out here; just itself, its hopes and dreams, its labs and guns; the several billion square hectares of ice on which its soldiers and scientists can play daily with their new toys.

You better listen when I tell you the Company creams its pants for real estate like this. And when the Company creams its pants, it's bail or drown for the rest of us.

You may have noticed I'm talking about the Company as if it were alive. There's a reason for that. Reckon I'll get round to telling it to you in a bit. Meantime, just show a little patience while I finish the window dressing. It's pretty spectacular; you can trust me on that. Leastwise there's a whole lot of toys involved. Some of 'em real hush hush, some not. In fact, one of them's so secret it doesn't know it even exists yet.

Let alone that it's alive.

Right at this moment this secret which lacks self-awareness is running at fifty kilometres per hour across the ancient ice of a shattered world, laser eyes scanning in the cloudy darkness, muscles pumping like metal jackrabbits, brain hardwired with psychosis-inducing adrenal surrogates.

It's the first of its kind. The first of a new breed. It's looking for something to kill.

It's just about to find you.

– 2 –

You're getting close to middle-aged. Too many good people around you have bought the farm. You want out. Out of the mission, out of the

2

military. You're getting old, you're desperate and pissed off.

But right now you've got a job to do.

You're a chopper pilot for Saggs Industries Military and you're hunting the Shadowman's new toy.

At least, that's what it wants you to think.

See it's like this: fact is you're dead already, you just don't know it yet. You were dead from the moment it activated. Well, born. Hell, either word'll do, I guess. In a pinch. Not that it really matters to you. You're in a pinch yourself right about now. As I said, you just don't realise it yet.

I can see you up there, oh, say fifty metres up, chasing ninety k.p.h., rotors chopping the grimy methane snow into mush, engines thumping the cockpit seat against your ass. You're dodging mountains, running canyons with guns hot, EM and radar eyes wide open, wetting yourself for a shot at the new toy. A shot and maybe a hit, and then maybe another shot, this time at some leave. Mars is at perihelion just about now. Get a hit and the prize money would pay for a week in Hogtown. A kill and there'd be enough to go home for a visit. Home. Earth. Jewel of the Solar System. Home of the teeming masses. Centre of government and art and society and history. Home of the only real trees and real beer and real women and real drugs in two hundred and fifty AUs.

Look at you. Jacked and eager. You want any and all of the above. Want it real bad. You've been running on emotional fumes for too long. As a man you're a machine; as a machine you're long past your sell-by date. Garrisoned with two hundred and forty nine others just like you, head full of dreams when it should have been full of tactics. Petty annoyances and personality clashes and fights in the bunkroom and a serious dose of out-system winter blues.

One thought and you might have made it. An extra moment's concentration on the chopper's instrument spread or a lucky gust of methane wind against the tail rotor and you might have made it home; might have had that holiday, laid with those women, guzzled that beer, taken those drugs.

Too bad.

Well, too bad for you. Great for Saggs. President-to-be Edward J. Saggs, that is.

E.J. Saggs: Company man, loyal bureaucrat, true blue through and through. It's his fault you're here. You don't know that of course. That's how he wants it. How he always wants it. He's the Shadowman. Self-styled mover and shaper of people and worlds. It's his will as much as anything which killed you.

Fact is, your deniable.

It's that simple.

Here's how you die:

You're hunting the new toy. It's hiding in the ice crevasses of the north polar zone. You're quartering the area with seven other choppers. They're blips on the radar; distorted voices in your helmet phones. Outside the canopy the air's a mess. Snow, squalls, ice cliffs crouching in the blue-stained darkness as if to leap and strike. Direct vision's a dead loss so you fly by wire; the blip's there, red hot, centred on the plate.

The new toy.

It's moving fast, running with the efficiency of a machine while using natural cover like an animal. And it's modulating its body heat. It's seen your infra-red. Christ the thing learns fast. Now it's hidden from one moment to the next, visible only as a moving squall pattern. Hidden, it still has mass: the wind has to move around it, the snow too. It's a whirlwind, a dervish careening across the torn ice.

You tell the chopper to loose a rocket, a heat-seeker; it's distracted by a geothermal vent, takes out the side of a mountain. Anaerobic life dies by the billions of particles. You fly through the debris, flame scarring the canopy, momentarily blinding you before being torn away by the wind.

You look for the results of the strike. A miss,

5

but the target is visible now, jigging sunward. It's out of hiding, sacrificing stealth for speed, heading for the terminator. The base. It's running home. It's running to ground.

You loose more missiles, hoping for a lucky strike or a disabling near miss. Unlucky, you chase the new toy into a box-canyon. Hover a thousand yards away as it fetches up against the rock wall of the canyon. Even the new toy can't burrow through an eighth of a mile of rock and ice.

You wait while it tries, then tell the chopper to bracket the toy's position and blow it to hell. You take a moment to signal a clean kill. Sure, it's anticipation but you've got to claim the kill now or miss your chance of collecting the prize money. There's kick-ass pride in your voice – and why not? Eight choppers and it was you who made the kill. You who'd be collecting the cash and heading for Earth.

Your finger's on the launch button when the night turns briefly into day. You lose it then; the chopper bucks like a live thing, smashing you against the restraint harnesses as

there's air, air in the cabin, pouring in through a hole in the canopy, a perfectly round hole which cuts cleanly through glass and dashboard and

the chopper punches into the side of a mountain. Rotors give it up as a dead loss and sud-

6

denly you're falling. Then the night flashes again and this time the hole is through the canopy, the dashboard, your chest, the seat. Way back in the engine cowling machinery coughs and screeches. Here in the canopy you do the same as the pain hits. It hits straight away, no messing, and you want to puke.

The cabin is on fire.

Outside the ground and the sky switch places.

Somehow the chopper stays with you. Built to kick ass or to save yours in a grounding the chopper hits ice burning. You're into shock by then, skin and eyes and lungs and throat burning from methane exposure, body jacked with adrenalin from puncture wound in your chest. There's blood in the suit, you can hear it sizzling in the heat from the electrical fires. You reach for the medikit; your arm won't move. Changing tack, you try for the eject handle: same story. Something is telling you there's no way out. Not this time.

The chopper melts its way into the ice. Liquid floods into the cabin. The fires are out by now, extinguished as the chopper tries to save itself.

For a moment you think you might make it. You try to reach the radio; cough blood instead. You try to move again, try to reach the canopy release, the medikit, the radio, the coffee flask wedged against the dashboard, any damn thing;

7

suddenly you're laughing, faced with the absurd image of yourself, waving madly as if from a holiday boat as the chopper sinks into the ice.

It gets cold real fast.

Your last thought is that the toy wasn't hiding, it was hunting: luring you into range for the kill. It was only born today but already it is smarter than you.

The last thing you see is ice forming on your helmet visor.

The last thing you feel is stupid.

The last thing you do is cry.

– 3 –

You're a hunterkiller; one link further up the chain of command than the pilot Saggs has ordered you to find. You float six feet above the ice in a military hovercraft, hot gunmetal steaming in the snow, EM and radar shut down. You have a feeling about this one. Pilots aren't stupid. They fly by wire – use every tool at their command. They rarely fail in their objective. Rarer still are they shot down and actually killed. Now this has happened and the Shadowman wants intelligence. He wants to know what the pilot did wrong. How the new toy took out a fifty mill stealth chopper and a pilot with eight years' experience in the field.

So he's sent you in with a ground battalion.

Four APCs, all blind and dumb at your command, all shovelling slowly forward on livesight only, hatches popped, navigators using passive night vision goggles to penetrate the driving snow and plastic comtubes to direct movement.

It's cold – no-one complains. They're too well trained, too disciplined, unlike the pilot. Privately you dislike pilots. Undisciplined rabble. In your head three centuries of airforce-ground-force rivalry hammers. You are better.

You *are* better; you are alive. Not that you're going to be that way for long. But there it is. Nobody's perfect.

The APCs slow as the chopper looms out of the dimness. Only the top half is visible, rotors gone, engine cowling scorched and twisted, the forward part of the fuselage and nose instrument package buried in solid ice. Two holes have been drilled – no, melted through the airframe. From the angle of exit both obviously penetrate the cabin – one emerges from the canopy, the other from the rear of the engine cowling. The tail rotor has been truncated, as if something incandescent passed close by as it was spinning. You have never seen damage like this.

There's no smoke, no steam; only a small hot spot delineates the chopper from any other irregular lump of snow-covered terrain.

There's no sign of the pilot.

9

You order the APCs to slow and spread out. You shout above the wind to do this. You tell them to maintain visual distance and use black-light morse to communicate. No live signals, no EM, nothing; silent running until the target moves and the guns get hot.

You ignore the chopper. Time enough for intelligence when the new toy is dead.

You are careful. Very careful.

You hope it will make a difference.

The APCs move to circle the half-buried chopper at your command. You peer through the murk, night goggles set to full gain. Beads of blacklight glimmer in the darkness. The APCs, talking to one another. You scan the immediate surroundings. Cold and dark – just the blacklight talking and the hot spot formed by the wrecked chopper's fast-cooling engine.

No sign of movement. No sign of life.

You search the canyon walls.

Nothing.

Even the new toy cannot mask its output totally. Unless it is dead. Either the toy has moved on or the chopper took it out in the crash. A suicide run for the pilot. Mutually assured destruction.

You order the APCs to cover your approach to the chopper. The Shadowman wants informa-tion. Your job is to get it.

You are fifty yards from the wreck and the engine is cooling fast now. Just one last hot spur, pulsing among the debris, and even that is fading faster than an ice cube in a belly dancer's –

Wait a minute.

The hot spot isn't fading. It's constant.

It's *moving*.

It's –

hiding the fucking thing's hiding in the dead chopper and it's hiding and waiting for you and hunting you and

breaking EM silence you scream instructions into the pickup. The APCs are moving in an instant. They're fast. Very fast.

Not quite fast enough.

The night flashes. Threads of fire bisect the darkness and the APCs are history. You hear screams truncated by the sizzle of burning flesh before the comm-lines go down. Shrapnel from three messy explosions shreds the ground nearby.

You barrel down the hatchway into the APC as the night splits again and again. You are a hunterkiller, one of the best, and you know how to move. You are fast. Very fast.

Like the APCs you aren't quite fast enough.

The first pulse overloads your night goggles and welds your arm to the raised hatch. The second punches a hole in the hatch and takes off your left leg. Blind, in shock from the amputation and holding back a scream by sheer bloody-mindedness, you order a targeting solution on the chopper.

The guns move randomly, searching for a target.

Your pickup is dead, the gunner hasn't heard you.

You scream then.

The third pulse cuts the APC in half and you along with it.

– 4 –

Your name is Gerome Nabel and you are the father of the Shadowman's new toys. You work in the equatorially situated DNA COBRA laboratory complex. The lab is a fortress. You call it the Hill and it is a hill, one made of metal and plastic, stone and glass, superconductors and organic liquid computers.

It is a sponge for money and human lives.

At this moment you are on your way to the operations room. Soldiers and scientists run in confused patterns throughout the warren of corridors and labs. Not you. You are calm. Precise of thought and spare of movement. You do not share their panic, their fear. And why should you? You have created what they most fear.

12

The new toy that the Shadowman is even now playing with.

As yet the new toys do not have a name. A name defines an identity. The new toys have no identity as yet, though they will develop them with time. The Shadowman doesn't know that yet. But then he knows very few of your secrets. You smile, a thin, confident compression of the lips, entirely lacking warmth and humour. The Shadowman is confident in his ignorance. And that is how you like it. Confidence breeds mistakes and anyone prone to mistakes is controllable.

And make no mistake, if there is one thing you have learned over the many years of your life it is that God and luck are cruel and merciless, and that any natural advantages must be developed and utilised to their best effect as fast as possible. Anything else is tempting fate; a waste of life.

Waste is your demon; the one thing you find truly abhorrent.

The operations room is an almost matchless example of waste; redundancy and repetition are the watchwords here. After three years on Triton you are beginning to think the military should have them emblazoned on an official motto.

Or inscribed with blunt kitchen knives into their genitals.

The operations room is large, semicircular,

13

accessed by wide double doors of six-inch-thick blast alloy. Glimmering designer consoles fit snugly into the alcoves which surround the room. Too many consoles, too many alcoves. The curved wall is filled with monitor screens. Too many screens. All are activated. Some are flickering with static or tracer fire. Five are dark. Console operators move in their depressingly familiar, triply redundant patterns throughout the room. They surround a central dais on which is a master console and a padded chair. The chair is very large and squashy. It is filled to capacity with a very large, squashy man.

Edward J. Saggs.

The Shadowman.

You grin inwardly at the size of his ass. The grin widens as you calculate the percentage of ass which actually overhangs even such a large chair. Then he turns ponderously to stare at you and the grin shrivels. As a man he is little more than a transport mechanism for sagging skin and heavy bones, a great deal of fat, a rather leaner portion of intelligence; yet still his gaze inspires everything from awe to terror.

At least that's what it inspires in the staff. In you it inspires fascination. The Shadowman is a bug. An exotic life-form to be studied and from which much may be learned. At the very least the Shadowman is one rung on the ladder of achievement – your achievement. And he doesn't even know it.

When he speaks his voice is controlled, an actor's voice. It calls to mind the clichéd image of a vid-star or out-system pioneer.

His voice, like his words, lies cleverly. 'Nabel. I expected you here sooner.'

Of course you did you fat sack of shit. 'A small delay in the programming sector. A minor deviation in the hatcheries. Nothing more. Certainly nothing to worry about.'

The Shadowman nods, satisfied. You smile, turn to study a monitor to cover the gesture. A man whose ambition outstrips his learning is easy to please, easy to fool.

'Five deaths. There have been five deaths.'

'A pilot, a hunterkiller and four million in hardware.' The Shadowman smiles suddenly, and you get an image of children screaming. 'Rather a good tally, wouldn't you say?'

You nod. Human life is incidental, the war machines less so. They were paid and came knowing the risks of the game. Play and fight. Fight and die. Winner takes all. Everything is deniable.

The new toy is performing well.

Attention in the room shifts suddenly as another monitor goes black. The audio link to Chopper Five lasts a little longer, bringing screams and a terrible crackling before going dead.

A console operator half turns, careful not to catch the Shadowman's eye. 'Artillery pattern suggests new target vector at ground zero.'

The Shadowman snaps a response. 'Confirm!'

Confirmation comes as more monitors flicker and die amid screams and flames. Suddenly the room is full of voices.

'Intrusion countermeasures activated.'

'We just lost Command Seven.'

'Tac-com indicates perimeter seven has been penetrated.'

'Confirm. Breach in progress. Killzone narrowing.'

'Deploy Beta squad, full spread. Get the net out, now, and fry that bastard!'

You stand among the controlled chaos, rigid. A half-smile plays about your lips, allowed full expression as the final monitors blip into static, each one representing a half-dozen lives spent to protect the Hill from the new toy.

'It's coming home.' The Shadowman licks his lips. 'Well, Nabel, I expected more and I got it. You are to be congratulated.'

You meet the Shadowman's eyes, allow yourself a moment of quiet satisfaction. 'It isn't over yet.'

'Oh?' Is that a quiver in his voice? Fear? Anticipation? The thrill of the challenge? 'Seal the Hill!'

In seconds the room is full of troops and the blast doors are rolling shut. Distant rumbling crashes tells of more heavy doors clanging into place to secure the Hill from breach.

Five minutes pass. Ten.

Nobody moves. Nobody speaks.

At least – nobody does or says anything intelligent or sensible.

Not until the tech-squad get the monitors online in time to watch Chopper Nine take a hit and crash squarely on to the uplink dish. The pilot bails out. Not that it makes any difference. He is toast in the air, visible for a moment as a bright spurt of flame in the dirty snow.

More monitors fire up. The troops have surrounded the Hill.

The new toy comes through them like a wind through trees, silent, invisible, traceable only by the corpses it leaves melting holes in the ice in its wake.

You are not surprised when the outer wall is breached. You are watching the Shadowman. He is impassive. The distant screams and hammer of gunfire leave him unmoved.

Door after door follows the outer wall into slag. The new toy is moving so fast the monitors cannot keep up. Soon there is no more gunfire, no screams.

A moment of silence.

The blast doors fold inwards like wet tissue paper.

It is here.

You do not need to see it to know its anatomy, the way it moves. It is a hunter. It is here to kill. It will kill everyone in the room if it can. It was born and bred to fight and it knows more ways to kill than a Samurai warrior crossed with a fission bomb. It is 101 per cent efficient. There are no mistakes. No get-out clauses. No fuckups.

It is here. It is real. It is the prodigal returned.

It steps delicately over the slushy remains of the blast doors.

Nobody moves. The console operators are in shock, the troops are assessing the target, waiting for orders.

The Shadowman is watching intently, fascinated.

He makes a signal. The first wave of troops open fire. About five thousand rounds. They shred the remains of the door and take out part of the corridor wall beyond.

Unmoved, the new toy turns its head and gazes at them.

A flicker of light and the troops are gone to a man, bodies knifesliced off at mid shin and vaporised, leaving a neat row of steaming boots to topple like slow dominoes, flesh and blood bubbling from the shin-snaps.

18

The new toy gazes around the room.

It is that fast. The blink of an eye and only you and the Shadowman are left alive. There is no time even to panic.

A blur of motion and the new toy is standing over Shadowman, poised to deliver the Medusa gaze. Shadowman looks at you. He knows he is going to die. He looks at you. The new toy looks at him.

You use the operator remote and deactivate it.

The Shadowman scrambles to his feet, prods the deactivated toy, blinks heavily up at the three lustreless grey eyes. 'This exercise is concluded. Security, stand down.'

Predictably, no-one responds.

Shadowman holds out one trembling hand for the operator remote. You hand it over without question. 'How many people know about this, Nabel?'

'I'm the only one with the whole picture, Mister Saggs.' You cast a quick glance around the carnage which is the operations room and add proudly, 'Now.'

'It was expensive. A high investment. I shall expect a high return.'

'Of course, sir.'

It doesn't take much imagination to see the potential here. 'With enough of these little . . . toys . . . I could take over the world.'

19

The musing is a vanity, one which you delight in taking seriously. 'Which world, sir?'

'Why Earth of course. The government's been hanging by a thread for years. And why leave all that fine history, art and culture to plebeian grounders who cannot possibly appreciate it as you or I can?'

'Indeed.'

'Why should we be paying taxes when we could be collecting them – and run the government ourselves with a twenty per cent improvement in the culture–finance ratio? With a hundred of these –' You touch the warm metal skin of the new toy reverently '– we could remodel the slum areas, slim down the inappropriate population, weed out the genepool, we could . . .'

You smile. This time you allow him to see it.

'How many? Nabel?' There is excitement in his voice. That and anticipation. 'How many new toys have you made for me?'

You lick your lips. 'Five thousand are waiting in the incubators to hatch.'

'I'm impressed. And these creatures, they . . . think? Actually think? For themselves?'

'I call it unified cognition.'

'I am sure you do, Nabel. What does it mean?'

You step to one side, slip in a puddle of solider, regain your balance with an embarrassed gasp.

'Well, Mister Saggs, they're a mass mind. A gestalt. They think like one being. Each learns from the others' experiences.'

'Again, I'm impressed.' Shadowman notes the still-bubbling fat on his chair and decides to remain standing. 'Tell me more.'

'They can live in a vacuum by conversion of direct sunlight. They are invisible to conventional EM detectors. Invisible in darkness. Their armour is capable of mimetic function – uh, except when switched off of course, as now. They can outrun a military hovercraft and jump high enough to catch a chopper at fifty metres. They are light. You could lift this one with one hand. It's a new alloy. A memory metal. They live hard and learn fast and . . . that's the broad spec. We're still developing the fine details.'

'And they kill.'

'Oh yes. Each has a particle beam weapon built into the skull chassis.' You smile proudly and rub your hands together. 'There's nobody within five years of having anything remotely like it.'

Shadowman holds out the operator remote. 'And this?'

'Turns them on and off. Directs them. I have others. This particular unit has your voice assigned primary command authority.'

The Shadowman turns the device over in his fat hands.

For the first time he smiles.

For the first time in your life you know fear. Just a shadow, slipping across your soul. A moment and you dismiss it as errant fantasy. No base in reality. The Shadowman needs you. And anyway – you are the father, the creator. They are your toys as much as his, aren't they?

Well – aren't they?

The Shadowman speaks again. His voice is full. Resonant and charming. One imagines babies being kissed from a presidential car.

'You're a genius, Nabel. I'm proud of you. The company is proud of you. And if circumstances permitted I'd green light a hellacious great bonus and promotion for you on the spot – but, our objective on Earth – you can see how that precludes any such bonus, I am sure.'

'Well, as a matter of fact –' You stop. Fear is blooming fast now, overwhelming. Yet with it, a curious calm. A sense of displacement. As if you are not really here. And something else. Yes, a sense of *destiny*. As if this is all quite inevitable.

'Of course you do, Nabel, clever man like yourself. Genius like yourself. Of course you see. You see what has to be. And of course this all has to be deniable.'

A look from those deeply pouched yet penetrating eyes.

'From which you may safely infer that you, too, are deniable.'

Shadowman caresses the operator remote.

He turns on the new toy and tells it what to do.

You don't run.

The look on your face as the new toy turns its Medusa gaze on you is little short of ecstasy.

– 5 –

You are the Shadowman. You are the *Shadowman* and you are *alive*. Every breath tells you so, every rank, steaming inhalation of the stench of scorched uniform and cooking bacon-fat which is all that remains of your men, every eye-stinging splutter of dead electrical circuits, every dripping puddle of molten metal which had once been multi-billion dollar state-of-the-art technology.

All gone.

Gone in a blink.

All down to Nabel.

And the new toy.

You stare at the new toy. It towers over you. Two and a half metres. Chitin black. A sponge for light. Insectile and at once human-like. Everything about its lines and its movement spells out O.R.G.A.N.I.S.E.D. D.E.A.T.H. in hostile capitals. Everything from its design to its growth rate to its violence to its learning curve is utterly without parallel, at once terrifying and exhilarating.

It is yours.

It is your new toy.

You tell it what to do next.

You tell it to kill.

– 6 –

You are the Shadowman's new toy. His voice is your god. His pleasure is your joy. You cut the maker in half at his command. You destroy the laboratory complex and everyone in it at his command.

You go to sleep at his command.

And wait.

Hogs

– 1 –

Your name is John Canyon. You're a Space Trucker. You're as pissed as a three-legged dog and puking on your own grave.

The grave is located on Mars, on the bumpy lava shield of Olympus Mons, overlooking the sprawl of Hogtown and the spaceport. The thought of the port makes you puke again. A genuine Martian multicoloured yawn, splashed right across your headstone.

The name on the stone isn't yours, of course. At least not any more. It's your old name. The name you gave up when you died. The name you are here paying your last respects to.

You wonder if dying was a mistake. You gave up your old life when you did that. Some would say fifty-four is too old to start over.

Then again what the hell would they know about it?

You take another slug of Castlemaine XXXX. It's the only poison in town – but it'll do to bury yourself with. You lose your balance as you gulp it down. That leaves you with no breath in the thin air. You grab for your gravestone, miss by a mile and end up sitting in the puddle of vomit you have just made.

Your heart hammers.

Old heart.

Old rig.

New life.

You stare up at the diamond sky arching overhead. Machines glimmer distantly as they move to and fro, repairing holes torn by the odd asteroid collision.

You blink. Take another slug. Remember your own collision with that barrier. Jesus H. Christ on His great steel wheels, that landing was hard. The hardest you have ever made. But it was easy as slipping in mud compared to what happened afterwards.

The trouble began six months ago on the back of an Earth–Mars run, when your rig and best friend *Bitchin' Betty* developed an unhealthy blockage in her primary ramscoop soon after entering Mars orbit.

That's not unusual in itself: anyone'd tell you there's all sorts of shit floating around in space. There's rock and sand and gravel, junk older than the Solar System. There's metal scrap: bits of old space shuttle, dysfunctional satellites, jacked corpses; in fact all kinds of rubbish from nearly three centuries of spaceflight. There's terrestrial shit and non-terrestrial shit and all of it'd kill you, most like, if it hit you going fast enough.

Thing is, if you were a betting man – which you are, and a fine one at that – even you wouldn't have taken long odds that in the whole Solar System the thing that was going to cost you your rig, your girl, your load of Interpork hogs and, on one occasion at least, your life, was nothing more or less than a Castlemaine XXXX six-pack with a single unopened can of beer still attached.

Mind you, the odds on that bet might've been shorter if you'd known that can of XXXX was moving through the big dark on a precision course with *Bitchin' Betty*'s fuel lines.

Right then, though, you were not concerned with betting. Unusual, but there it is. You were more concerned with the fact that *Betty*'s fuel-injection system was having a major party without your permission and without inviting you along. The stick was a limp dick in your hand and *Betty* herself was a dead weight churning down out of a pink sky towards the surface of Mars – a surface which you've since learned can be as cold and hard as an Eskimo's bed when you are sitting on it, let alone when you are a dead weight of eighteen hundred metric tons falling at sub-orbital velocity.

You made it down in one piece by using the

HOKAI Corporation's sixteen trailers of frozen hog-sperm, which you were hauling, as a heat shield.

The HOKAI Corporation were pretty mad at that. Six months' very expensive high-grade Research and Development had gone into the production of those DNA sequences, and the fact that they had just saved your life was as nothing compared to the fact that a whole generation of highly lucrative hoglets would never, now, be anything more than a mote in God's eye.

The HOKAI Corporation lawyers sued your ass, and your ass was just what they got. Your ass and your rig – repaired and indentured to the HOKAI Corporation for as long as they wanted it. A company slave for the rest of your life.

Well, you weren't having that. There was nothing else for it but kill yourself. They'd understand that: ritual suicide. And if they didn't then the insurance company with which the HOKAI Corporation doubtless insured their loads certainly would.

So you waited until weather conditions were right and a major sandstorm was carving up the plains, and you suited up and you took a walk out of Hogtown. You found a rock, sat down, took out a stylus and pad and began to write.

Hog farmers found you about a week later, suit breached, body eroded beyond recognition by sandstorms, suicide note glued to the inside of your visor.

The note had HOKAI Corporation executives bawling in their boardroom. They had a minute's silence for you and then ordered a (tax deductible) monument to your pioneering spirit erected beside the (workers') entrance to their Earth offices.

Their insurance claim went through like cod-liver oil through a hog.

It took half your life savings to buy a new name and passport. It took the rest to buy *Bitchin' Betty* back from the local scrap dealers and repair her. Then there was the little matter of a livelihood. That was harder. You spent half a year gambling to raise enough of a stake on a new cargo. Half a year in bars where the only beer was Triple XXX, the IQ averaged one point lower than your shoe size, and where even the classiest barmaid couldn't hold an electric candle to Cindy.

Half a year of shit company and shit beer and just shit-in-general. But you bulled on through because you had no choice. You got your new name and a new cargo and your old rig back.

And that, though you don't realise it yet, is the exact moment when your troubles really began. Because if you can't lift for Mars orbit within six hours you might as well stay dead. Problem is,

29

staying dead costs money – costs a hell of a lot more than staying alive, in fact, owing to certain payoffs involved in setting up the deal – and you're flat broke.

Now, with a new cargo waiting to load and a delivery deadline in Saturn space close to expiry, you realise the whole kit-and-kaboodle is about to go to hell so fast it could have been shot there in a FedEx ballistic shuttle.

Because of the dockers' strike.

The Martian Labour Union announced the strike six hours before your cargo was due to load and it was one more turd on a planet-sized mountain of turds. It's not that you're not sympathetic. Sure, their pay is crap. Sure, their conditions are crap. Sure, there's more crap in a docker's life than there is in a bar-room toilet. But why in seven kinds of hell can't they wait just one more lousy Martian day before telling everyone in the system about it and pissing them off in the process?

You think about this as you pull yourself upright, puke once more for luck and stagger back through Hogtown towards the spaceport.

At least that's what you intend to do.

What actually happens is that you trip on a boulder, hit the ground snoring and stay that way for six hours.

When you awake the sun is rising. The night has buggered off. Jocund dawn sways drunkenly on the misty . . . something or other.

Shaking your head in a vain attempt to banish the hangover gibberish, you make good on last night's decision to head for town. At least you give it your best shot.

It takes three hours to reach town.

The heat and stillness of the port gets to you. This is the one place on Mars where you should be happy. The place should be hopping like a barndance – rigs laying dust, cranes chugging, trailers loading, dogs barking, riggers swearing. Instead the place is full of motionless rigs upended beside motionless trailers, surrounded by motionless cranes and even more motionless dock-riggers.

Realise this you get hotter, dustier, thirstier and angrier with every passing moment. It is no comfort at all that the only things moving are the thin clouds hugging the underside of the sky, and the dog that's taking a crap on your rig's passenger ramp.

To take your mind off it all you think about the cargo.

The signs on *Bitchin' Betty*'s cargo trailers read:

That's a hoot. They breed 'em square these days to fit in the cages. Some say they're doing the same to people – only not so's you'd notice.

Or maybe you do notice – if you haven't gone square yourself.

Talking of people, you look around in the vain hope that one of the picketing riggers might have a bottle of relatively clean H-two he'll want to sell, but all you can see as far as either pink, misty horizon are rigs and loaders and trailers – hundreds of trailers – and the odd dog pawing at the sealed containers.

You kiss the idea of a drink goodbye and stare instead at your rig. Five thousand square hogs in five thousand square cages in twenty office-block-sized trailers are stacked round *Bitchin' Betty*'s frame loader. That's a cool twenty-six grand by the time the load gets to Saturn space. Six grand of it profit. The gold at the ass-end of hell's friggin' rainbow.

Problem is, the only thing moving in Hogtown spaceport apart from the dogs is you – and the most effort you've made in the last two hours is to wipe the puke from the night before off your overalls.

You close your eyes, hoping that lack of motion in the spaceport is the result of a desert mirage or Castlemaine poisoning; when you open them again the loaders are still offline – though now the riggers are passing time by chucking bits of clinker from the engine tubes at the dogs to piss them off.

It's pissing you off too. Right about now everything in the wide pink yonder is pissing you off. The list seems endless: you're dead. You haven't seen your girl for months. You're not sure she'll still be your girl any more. Your last run was a grade-A disaster. There's a hole in your wallet to match those in your boots. You're still mostly wrecked from the night before. And of course that damn dog's still taking a crap on your rig's passenger ramp. Obviously it's got the shits.

And it's all down to those damn picketing dockers.

Even the dog having the shits is probably down to them as well.

You grab a load-rigger and tell him so, as loudly and obnoxiously as possible.

You're three days late and the hogs are starving and much more of this and you can kiss your profit goodbye in feed and overdue charges, and all of it down to these asshole mummies' boys and their asshole strike.

You tell him that, too. Also loudly and obnoxiously.

The rigger blinks in surprise, swears for a

whole minute without stopping and then calls you a blacklegger.

You look at your legs. By the time you've worked out he's landed a good right hook; you're up to your ass in alien sand and dogshit, and the tooth fairy's looking to make more profit out of the day already than you will in the next month.

You shake your head, pick up the nearest dog and throw it at the rigger. He takes it in the face and goes down. You wipe dogshit off your trousers, grind a handful into his face and ask him if he would care to comment on who is the blacker now?

His answer comes at the end of two-hundred and forty-pounds of pissed off muscle and bone.

You side-step the punch with drunken adroitness and he goes down again. You kick him for good measure: twice, once for each time he outweighs you.

The dog joins in the fight in time-honoured fashion.

You're splitting your sides at the rigger when six of his mates follow the dog into the fight. Mummies' boys every man Jack of 'em. They never learn.

The first two seem to get tangled around each other and fall, twin bruises already blooming where their skulls met briefly. The third stumbles on the first long enough for you to pick him up and throw him at the fourth, and that leaves you just enough time to grab a wheel-iron from the loader toolrack to deal with the last two.

Ten minutes later you are looking sadly down at all seven as the dog – bless him – comments again in the only way he seems to know how.

One of the riggers sits up. There is a bruise the size of an apple across his skull, one eye is black and blood trickles from his crushed nose. He reaches for his breast pocket and then squeals indignantly. 'Goddamn mutt stole my lunch!'

You look at the dog. It is worrying at the wrapper of an industrial-sized Mars bar. You laugh. The rigger misses the joke but looks pissed anyway. You say the magic doggie word and the mutt brings the Mars over to you and drops it at your feet. The riggers look impressed.

Shiner reaches for his lunch and suddenly the dog isn't wagging its tail – it's hunkered down and growling. Its teeth look very long and sharp and dangerous.

You stare at the rigger. 'Guess you've lost your lunch there, boy.'

The rigger scowls at the dog, who sits down two inches from the Mars bar with a little glance your way.

'Guess it cost you a mite, too, huh?'

Shiner glares sullenly.

35

'Shipping costs from Earth, use of an illegal stimulant – well. I guess the best you can do is hope my furry pal here gobbles down the evidence before that dock inspector I see ambling this way to check out the fight arrives.'

Shiner presses his lips together. Six heads turn to ascertain the truth of your words. The seventh divides his gaze between the mutt and his lunch. Ex-lunch.

'Course, I could always get it back for you.' You reach out and take the bar from the ground. Shiner's one good eye widens.

'Guess I could let you have it back, too. It's hardly scratched. Don't suppose the wrapper's even broke. You could wipe the doggie spit off it and it'd be good as new.'

Shiner says nothing.

'Course, that wouldn't be fair would it? Then you'd be getting something for nothing.'

Shiner spits out a tooth and says, 'What?' Actually he kind of spits out the word too. With lips as puffy and crusted with blood as his, that's no surprise.

'And since there's seven of you against the two of us, well –' You shrug, move as if to put the Mars bar back on the ground beside the dog, '– it'd hardly be fair to us, now would it.'

It isn't a question and you don't expect an answer.

You wait.

The dock inspector is two rigs away.

Forgetting his post-fight condition for a moment, Shiner bites his lips indecisively. Ignoring his painful whimper, you take back the Mars bar.

'On the other hand, we could play jacks for her. Winner takes the Mars, loser loads *Bitchin' Betty* here. I'll even let you have seven plays to my one, since there's seven of you. Whaddaya say, boys? Beats a spell in poke for trafficking stims, right?'

Shiner blinks his one good eye. You swear you see a tear in there.

'Ladies and gentlemen, that's the deal on the table. Whaddaya say?'

– 3 –

Black Eye and the other dockers agreed, as you guessed they might. *Betty* got loaded, the dog got the evidence as a snack and you got into orbit in record time.

Now here you are four days later entering Saturn space, marginally late, but pretty sure it's nothing you can't deal with in your own way. In fact, if you weren't such an experienced gambling man you'd be inclined to say that life was almost too good to be true. You have food, a job, one over on the Mars Dockers' Guild and an even bigger one over on the HOKAI Corporation – who, hopefully, still think you're dead.

As an extra bonus the surgery performed on your rig is also performing outstandingly. *Betty* is tearing up the spacelanes like there's no next week.

You don't know it yet but for *Betty*, at least, there won't be a next week.

But you don't know that and if you did you'd probably think it was a whole pile of space opera. You're John Canyon and you're feeling pretty damned alive for a dead man. Right about now you're manning the driver's pit, happily playing null-g docking manoeuvres with a tube of mustard and a freight-load of Aussie 'roo-burgers. You have one hand on the stick, one eye out the wraparound windscreen, and the whole rest of your attention on the food hovering between you and the big dark. Pretty soon you're gonna have to apply some negative acceleration – *brakes* to you and me – and then the mealtime fun and games'll be over for a while. But till then you're happy as a bear in a honeypot with the three thoughts in your head: you have food in your belly, freight in your rig . . . and the prospect of seeing Cindy again for the first time in half a Martian year.

Cindy.

You think about her as the great bloated donut

of Saturn's ring system swims into view ahead; draw a picture of her in your head that has the 'roo-burger drifting, ignored, until it splashes down unnoticed against the afterburner sub-systems touchscreen.

Cindy.

You think about her for a moment – until StellarCom opens up a channel and squawks at you.

'I say again, this is SkyTown Traffic-Controller to incoming rig: state your goddamn ident and, for cryin' out loud fella, put the brakes on before you take out the goddamn mooring ring, willya!'

You blink. Sure enough, SkyTown is growing fast in the windscreen, a mountain-sized accu-mulation of battered airtights bolted together around a two-mile-wide multilevel ring-frame.

Betty bleats a warning then. SkyTown is clear and centred on the screen. Much too centred, in fact.

You open up a channel of your own. The smile in your voice is like a beacon in the big dark. 'Hey, honey, Daddy's home. This is John Canyon riding heavy freight Pachyderm Kilo Foxtrot one-niner-zero, otherwise known as *Bitchin' Betty*, and we're bringing all you stay-at-homes more square hogs than you all know what to do with. So I reckon you'll want to get us fixed

39

up with a docking berth as an A-1 priority – if you want to eat high for a year that is. Come on back to me, big guy.'

The Controller's voice is tired. '*Oh goddamn, we got ourselves a museum piece. Bay fifteen is clear, freight driver one-niner-zero, do you copy?*'

You smile. 'I surely do, good buddy, and I thank you for your help. Over and out.'

But docking isn't going to be that straightforward.

A new voice clicks into the traffic channel. '*Canyon, this is Bix Keller at Interpork Packers Dispatch. You're two days past due.*'

Your smile cracks a little. Keller. Oh how that man knows how to put a downer on the day. 'Hey, fat boy, it's been a while. Guess you haven't grown up none though. Tell you what, I'll just ditch these ol' relatives of yours and then we'll have us a drink and a bite to eat on the Company, OK?'

Keller is not amused. '*You just park your load and park your mouth, Canyon, you hear me?*'

The channel clicks dead.

You whistle with glee and whirl the stick. Attitude thrusters fire. SkyTown looms in the windscreen until it completely obscures the rather pretty view of half-full Saturn and three attendant moons. You're flying hot now, eyes half closed, matching the station's spin, winding *Betty* into the airing-cupboard space between four giant company supertrucks painted with glossy micrometeorite-repellent logos. Now you're sharing space with all sorts of hardware. Rigs, cranes, dock-loaders in spacesuits, bits of machinery, freight containers of all sizes, concession stalls selling everything from squeeze-tube 'roo-burgers to electrical spares, each complete with operator and neon logos blazing cheerfully out into the big dark.

You aren't quite able to repress a shout of glee as you stamp on the brakes. Retros screech briefly. A freight crane skitters out of the way, thrusters glimmering, as *Betty* rides in. You imagine the expression on the crane driver's face as fifteen hundred tons of slate grey, meteor-slashed Pachyderm freight-hauler gets on by him into the dock.

A screechy voice comes on to StellarCom. '*Kilo Foxtrot one-niner-zero, what the blue hell do you think you're doing? I just lost my goddamn lunch!*'

'You and everyone else I meet, buddy.' You throw the crane driver a cheery grin and a wave through the windscreen as you guide *Betty* one-handed into the dock with a flamboyant thump, setting off collision alarms right across the mooring ring.

SkyTown.

Oh yes.

You're John Canyon and you're *back*.

And this time you've brought back the bacon.

– 4 –

In space the food chain isn't so far from what it is on Earth. The only difference is, as a human, you're happy at the bottom of the pile instead of the top. See, it works like this: unhappy hogs make unhappy food, unhappy food makes unhappy accountants and unhappy accountants make unhappy Space Truckers. Simple, right? So it's in your interest to make sure your cargo is a happy one.

You tell *Betty* you want to go check on the hogs. She obliges by pressurising the freight crawlway between the trailers and opening the connecting hatch.

Leaving the mustard tube bouncing around the 'pit, you sling on some moonboots and the bottom half of a starsuit. Suit arms flopping drunkenly in the null-g, you clump back through the rig, through the kitchen and hammock space, towards the rear hatch. You pat your lucky dartboard as you go. Two clumpy steps later you rub dust from your lucky Gibson twelve-string. It's a little ritual you perform every time you leave or enter *Betty*. A good-luck thing.

Not that it's going to do you any good this time.

Another two steps and you're in the crawl-way.

Fortunately the hogs are fine. Little square faces in bi–i–i–ig square bodies in cages just big enough to hold them, cages stacked fifty deep in a cylinder around you, and which vanish away into the trailer in a perfect example of school-book perspective. Only one hog has puked – fortunately it's far enough away so that the smell hasn't reached you yet – and *Betty*'s autobutler is dealing with that.

Staring at the hogs, snuffling and hooting quietly to themselves and chugging on their food tubes, you suddenly lose your appetite. You toss the last of your 'roo-burger through the bars of the nearest cage. The hog noses fussily at the food before starting to nibble.

You watch until the burger is completely consumed. There. Get a little Canyon spit into the food chain.

As you watch, you talk to the hogs. 'Howdy, ladies and gentlemen. Guess by now you all probably realise where we are. Halfway to the end of the line for most of you. A little process-ing, a little packing, a few electric shocks, not necessarily in that order, and your journey will continue. In the mean time the Company will be

43

pleased to play you some relaxing music to make your wait more enjoyable.'

You tell *Betty* to play a little Emmylou Harris.

The hogs snuffle a little louder, responding interestedly to your voice, and to the music.

You are just about to join in with the chorus of 'Tenessee Tulip' when a distant clang and hiss breaks the peace. *Betty* shivers. The hogs shuffle nervously. They've got used to *Betty*. The noise of the connecting umbilical is foreign. You calm them down with the magic hog word, just like you did the dog on Mars.

That's better. 'Well, ladies and gentlemen. Everybody happy now?'

'No!' The new voice was preceded by the heavy footsteps of a man unused to null-g.

You grin knowingly. Misguided, uneducated fools of the kind who think hogs are ugly will say Bix Keller's voice is more like a pig's than a man's. It's high and screechy, exactly the way it came out of the StellarCom channel a few minutes before. Those same uneducated un-aes-thetically-appreciative fools might also describe Keller as resembling a tough, short-legged, square-chested porker himself. In both these descriptions they'd be quite right, insult to prized members of the food chain notwith-standing.

You turn. Keller, flanked by a pair of freight

handlers, is just stepping into the freight trailer. You know Keller from experience, the handlers by reputation. They are, respectively, Jackie: young and vicious, and Mel: old and evil.

You have to get the first word in, establish the pecking order. 'Well, looky here. My old friend Bix Keller and two of the warmest, friendliest sons you could want to name after girls, all come to inquire after the well-being of their relatives.' You pause long enough to nod towards the nervously snuffling hogs, then cut across Keller just as he starts to speak. 'You know, ladies, way back on Earth in the good old days of the twentieth century there was a theory that said hogs were intelligent. Clean and intelligent. Guess they bred that outta them, huh? Still, not to worry. You can't miss what you never had, am I right, or am I right?'

You stare right at Keller as you speak. He misses the personal dig, same as he always does. The girls just look puzzled. Well, Mel looks puzzled. Jackie's expression doesn't change by even a single millimetre.

Giving in to the inevitable, you bring the conversation down to a level you hope Keller will understand. 'So, where's my beer and when do I get paid?'

Keller is staring past you at the hogs. True family resemblance there. 'You can unhook your rig. Stop by my office in an hour and I'll cut you a check.'

You'd've had to have been born blind not to see that one coming. 'I'll unhook my rig when I've got my money.'

'You know that's not Company policy.'

The line was old when you were born and better men than Keller have tried to hide behind it. 'You're damn right I do. That's why it's my policy not to unhook before I'm paid.'

Keller sighs. Has he deliberately missed the ice in your voice or is he just stupid? Probably the latter. For Keller, being stupid is apparently not so much a job as a way of life. 'You're late, Canyon. Plenty late. Your tardiness idled men and machines, cost the Company money.'

You shake your head. 'You want I should apologise? Sure. I'm sorry. But you knew the score when you signed the contract. The hogs are here and they're happy.' You turn to address the cargo in question. 'Ain't that right, ladies and gentlemen?'

The hogs snuffle happily.

'See? You speak the same language, Keller. Listen to your peers. Happy hogs make happy food and happy food makes happy accountants. You and I both know what happy accountants make.'

'Sure I do. They make money. And they don't

do it by cutting slack.' Keller licks his lips. 'Canyon, the Interpork Accounts Department has authorised me to pay you fifteen hundred for these hogs.'

You try unsuccessfully to stifle a laugh. 'Why Mister Keller, I do believe you've grown a sense of humour in my absence. These hogs are worth six thousand, plus shipping costs of twenty thousand. Which adds up to a grand total of twenty-six thousand. That's what the deal was for; that's what you owe me.'

Keller steps forward, ducking beneath a row of crated hogs. The girls back him up. 'You don't seem to get it. I only negotiated the fifteen hundred out of impulsive generosity. I'm likely to withdraw the offer if it's not accepted gratefully and immediately.'

Your eyes narrow. You can feel them shutting down. You put every ounce of mean you have into the stare. 'I think it's time for you to leave, Mister Keller. You're upsetting my hogs.'

Keller chews on his lip for a moment, thinking. He makes a sound rather like a hog when he does this, thus proving his genetic heritage for all time. 'Mel, Jackie. Explain the situation to Mister Canyon will you?'

You remain still as the girls move. You watch their feet, the way their bodies move, the way they connect with the deck and wall rigging. Mel

47

hangs back. Sensible. Jackie springs forward, fist loaded, ready to fire. He's cocky and that's going to cost him some.

Hooking your toes under the null-g netting which lines the crawlway, you duck fast. Jackie misses his punch, goes sailing over your head. You slap an ankle as he passes and suddenly he's pinwheeling in place, three feet off the deck, too surprised even to squeak. Your hand on the back of his neck stops him spinning.

'I shouldn't really be explaining the facts of life to you. But you're young, so I guess you can have this lesson for free. You don't throw a punch that way in null-g. This here's the accepted technique.'

Locking your feet against the null-g netting you deliver a left hook which has Jackie pinwheeling down the crawlspace like a defective Chinese rocket, spitting curses and blood and two broken teeth into the air along the way. He fetches up against the bulkhead divider with a yell of pain and a clang that makes the nearest hogs squeal in terror.

Ignoring Jackie, you turn. 'Any more for any more?'

Mel has pulled a sidearm.

Keller slaps it aside contemptuously. 'What the blue hell you playing at?'

You assume Keller is talking to Mel. You're right.

48

'Bastid hit my bro'. Gon' kill him.'

You save your breath, let Keller explain it to Mel. 'You'd have better luck shooting him with your dick. Put it away before you depressurise the trailer and kill all of us.'

Mel scowls but does as he's told.

By this time the hogs have calmed down. Jackie regains his equilibrium and pushes past you, face split in a scowl which almost disguises how ugly he is. 'Gon' get you, you bastid,' he lisps bloodily as he draws level.

You grin. 'And just how much you reckon I got to fear from a coupla girls who can only use one word between them of more than one syllable?'

For a moment Jackie looks like he's going to lose it again. Keller saves the day with a moment of unprecedented common sense.

'Leave it, boys.' They do. 'But remember what I said, Canyon. You got one hour to unhook and I'll cut you a check for the fifteen hundred. Any longer and there'll be a reckoning between us. Remember, these hogs are Company property.'

You let a little more ice into your voice. 'These hogs belong to me until you pay me. Now get the hell off my rig.'

Thankfully, they get.

You're about to shut the hatch when something sharp and wet nudges the back of your neck. You grab it and hurl it after the retreating figures. 'And take your goddamn teeth with you!'

– 5 –

SkyTown is a junkers' town. It had been conceived as the first in a series of way stations spread throughout the slightly more civilised areas of the Solar System. The bad news was that after about fifty years or so of humans being in space there weren't any civilised areas any more. Just about everywhere you cared to name there were boondocks and badlands and jackers' parades.

SkyTown had originally been parked outside the rad belts in Jupiter-space. The first Marshall of SkyTown – man name of Singleton – soon put paid to that. He'd been in the job less than a year when he fired up the station-keeping engines and just moseyed on outta there. He brought SkyTown to Saturn, declared independence, set up what was then only the second nation state to be formed off the Earth – and was promptly killed by some loon who decided that 'independence' meant 'no law'.

This socially dysfunctional low-life whom legend sensibly allows to remain nameless was spaced sure enough – they saved his sorry-ass, space-bleached skull as a trophy for the Marshall's office doors, where it hangs to this day – and Singleton's second-in-command took over the job. From then on things ran smoothly. Half a century of growth had SkyTown as big as a mountain with more rings than a pack of donuts and inhabitants from more states and nations that you could name with the aid of a computerised Atlas.

Physically, SkyTown looks a mess. There are rings upon rings, different gravity systems, null-g zones, passenger and trading locks, a huge mooring ring which straddles the entire station. It shouldn't work but it does. It should have disintegrated years before just under its own bizarre inertia, but it hasn't.

And in a Solar System rapidly going to the dogs, as it were, SkyTown is the hub of it all. No-one gets anywhere, in- or outsystem, without going through SkyTown. It's a refuel dump, a trading centre, a rest house, a whorehouse. It's got hotels and hovels, it's got hydrobays and hydrobars and burger joints and strip joints. It's got autoshops and electrical suppliers and ring after ring of offices for just about every trading company registered for tax and VAT in nine planets and twenty-some moons.

Not to mention the ones that aren't registered.

It's also cornered the strip on black market goods, illegal trade, shady deals and downright thievery. Since SkyTown is a free town everyone goes armed and no-one can be arrested, evicted or generally messed about by the long arm of Terran Law. Well, leastways, not instation, anyway. Instation the Companies run their own little territories and the Marshall – old Marshall Compton Mbotumi – makes sure nobody gets shot who shouldn't. Usually.

A damn fine idea when there's folk like Bix Keller and his girls poking their noses in where they aren't wanted.

Right about now you've locked up *Betty* good and tight, set the cattleprod and moseyed on out in search of company and food. Specific food and specific company – finding anyone and anything amongst the mess that is SkyTown is an acquired skill. Fortunately you have it by the bucketload.

The trick with SkyTown is never to assume there's a pattern to anything but just to go with the flow. It's a place where gut instinct'll get you where you're going faster than any map. In this case you follow your nose, starting at the imaginatively named 'Food Ring' and from there tracking the smell of 'roo-burgers and ketchup through a quarter-mile of different sections and a hundred different types of hungry consumer, until you find what you're looking for.

You find her in the Space-Ring Burger Bar.

She'd dressed like a rodeo-girl.

She's just as beautiful as you remember.

Cindy.

Holy God on His great steel wheels, the woman is hot. She's hotter'n plasma and prettier than a solar eclipse and hornier than the horniest barchick ever. She's a woman to give things up for. A woman you want to make happy and then happier still. A woman worth more than every paycheck you've ever drawn. Even the one with the zero-misprint worth a quarter mill you cashed and just about got away with nearly a decade before Cindy was born.

Cindy. She's hot, she's beautiful, she's sensitive, she's loud, she's funny, she's smart as a whip and if cloning were possible you'd order up a dozen to go. With mayonnaise.

Sure she's young enough to be your kid. Just makes her that little bit more grateful to receive birthday presents, that's all.

You remember her seventeenth birthday then, and smile.

She's standing beneath the bar logo – a neon Saturn-globe girdled by the mother and father of all onion rings – serving some male eye-candy with a plate of stewed 'roo and – you guessed it – onion rings. You shift your weight nervously from one foot to the other. It's been half a Martian year. She might not even remember you. She doesn't notice you. A moment goes by and she continues not to notice you.

'Uh . . . Cindy.' The words come out kinda slow. 'Hiya.' Two syllables. Better than Mel and Jackie. Just.

She turns then. She recognises you.

It takes you five minutes to wipe the stewed 'roo from your face.

'Well, whaddaya know, it's John Canyon, the glamour guy of the gas pedal. Hiya John. Thought you'd swing past my way didya? Hell it's only been a year. A whole year John, with no you, no message, no nothing. Well I guess that's a message in itself, ain't it? Well I got it OK, you can believe that.'

You pull an onion ring off your ear. 'Cindy. I can explain.' You whirl the onion ring absently around your finger until it disintegrates.

Cindy flounces back to the bar and orders another meal for Mister Eye-Candy, currently eyeing you up with some amusement. 'No need. We're through. We were through before we started. I assume that's OK with you since I haven't seen you since I was practically in diapers?'

You grin. 'Girl, you're still practically in diapers. But I still love ya anyway . . .'

Your attempted joke falls flat. Women. You can't con them like dockers or punch them out like cops. You have to stand there and take it. And boy can they dish it out.

Sure as your old ma's temper, Cindy dishes you out another plate of 'roo. Quick as a whip, you dodge this one. Can't let them have more than the one over on you. The plate skims past your shoulder and hits a grease-monkey square in the chest. Mister Eye-Candy must think he's gonna starve unless you leave soon. Cindy vanishes behind the bar.

Time to slow things down.

You turn to the grease-monkey. 'Partner, I'm real sorry 'bout that. Why don't you have the next burger on the house? I'm sure they won't object since it was their staff what messed up those sparky coveralls you got there.' You wait for that to sink in, then add, loudly, 'Hell, if they won't stand you another meal, why I will, and you can thank John Canyon for that.'

The grease-monkey looks faintly embarrassed. Everyone in the bar – and that's a fair few – is looking at him now. He declines your offer, rams the last of his food into his mouth and makes off to change his clothes.

The situation is now under control. You mosey on over the Mister Eye-Candy and take a seat.

'Who're you?'

Eye-Candy offers his hand. 'Mike Pucci.'

Cindy was looking at this fellow. That makes your feelings about him mixed at best. 'Let's not get ahead of ourselves.' You decline the hand. 'What you say your name was? Puccini?'

'Pucci. Mike Pucci.'

'Yeah. You a Space Trucker, kid?'

'Not yet.'

'He's taking his solo today.' That's Cindy, back from the bar with another plate of stewed 'roo and onion rings for Eye-Candy, temper apparently forgotten. Emphasis on 'apparently'.

You shoot Cindy a glance.

Eye-Candy asks, 'What kind of rig you drive?'

Now there's a question a sensible man would ask. 'Pachyderm 2000.'

'Pachyderm . . . right.' The kid nods slowly. 'I guess you been driving a while.'

You don't like the turn this conversation has taken. 'Nothin' like that old iron, Mister Puccini.'

'Pucci.'

'Whatever.'

Overhead speakers crackle then, blasting almost incomprehensible nonsense over the hub-bub of the crowded bar. Eye-Candy looks nervously at the speakers.

'Waiting for something?'

'Got my solo today. Blow it and I gotta do forty more hours dual instruction in a trainer with a guy who don't wash under his arms.'

That you can sympathise with. 'Mister Purcell,

I do sympathise. But even if you do get your licence, there ain't a whole hell of a lot of jobs right about now.' You study the lad thoughtfully. "Less you plan to work for the Company, that is.'

Eye-Candy sticks his chest out so far you think he's about to beat it like some godforsaken monkey. 'I work for myself. But I ain't gonna let myself get all *agitato* about who signs the checks.'

The speaker crackles again. This time the words are clearly audible. '*Student Michael Pucci. Second and final call for student Michael Pucci. Report to mooring ring, low-side, area T.*'

Eye-Candy stands. 'Wish me luck, Cindy.'

She does that and then some. A kiss a man could drown in. Then he's gone, wobbling faintly with reaction. Or anticipation. Or both. You wonder which. Hell, you're gonna find out. It's only fair after all. So you do something really stupid. You ask her.

'Who's the kid? To you, I mean?'

You get a pointed look for your trouble. 'A customer. Like you.'

That hurts. 'I didn't use to be just a customer.'

Another look, this one unfathomable. How fast they learn to be women. 'What you having, John?'

You give it up for time being. 'I'm late. Keller

57

over at Interpork won't pay me. He figures I should feel lucky they're stiffing me.' You point to a nearby table. 'If you'll put it on the tab I'll have what they're having.'

Cindy's eyes narrow suspiciously. 'Habib might let me give credit on an ET burger.'

'I do not want an ET burger.' There's only so much shit a man will take. 'It tastes bad. It looks bad. It's probably been pissed on in the factory by the workers. You want I should go on?' You reach for the plate of stewed 'roo the kid left behind. Cindy's smarter; she goes for the fork, leaving you to consider eating from the plate or handing it back to her. A moment's face-off, then you hand back the food.

She's not sympathetic. 'New rules. All the leftovers get recycled.'

'Of all the cheap bullshit.'

Cindy turns abruptly and walks off, carrying the plate and food to the recycler. You feel like maybe you've missed something here. You get up and go after her, push through the crowded bar, ignoring the mixed looks you get. 'Hey. Hey, Cindy. What's the matter?'

For a moment she looks like she's going to push past you, then she stops, leans one hip against the recycler, bites her lip. 'I don't like it any better than you do, John. I just can't afford to lose my job. Especially now.'

You were right. There is something. Like a klutz you bull right ahead and ask what's up.

For a moment Cindy looks at you like she's going to take her best shot at your plug-ugly mug. Then she softens. 'My mother's on Earth, you knew that, right?'

Her mother? Her *mother*? 'You mighta mentioned, yeah.' You work hard to keep that puzzled tone out of your voice.

'Well, she's gotta have an operation, and, well, it's pretty serious, and I promised I'd be there with her.'

'That's pretty rough. I'm sorry. So when are you leaving?'

She laughs. Somehow there's less humour in that laugh than there is in one of Bix Keller's threats. 'You're joking right? You came all this way to laugh at me?'

'No, Cindy.' You think about reaching out for her. Wonder how hard she'll hit you if you've mistimed it. Decide to risk it anyway.

You touch her hand. Smooth skin. Warm. Electric tingle.

She doesn't shrug off your touch. Not exactly. Just sort of slides sideways so the recycler gets between the two of you.

'Don't, John. I'm not ready to –. Anyway, you know what a ticket costs. I'd have to pull double shifts here for a year to earn my way out of here.'

59

You feel an ache in your gut then, like you've been winded by a punch or kicked in the balls. 'Let me ask around, see if I can't come up with something.'

A long pause. 'You're a good man, John. When you're here. You're good but you're not a Company man. They only give Earth runs to Company people. Not one of them has the balls to risk taking me along.' A sigh. You see her go away then, somewhere inside, somewhere in some childhood memory of her mother, maybe the last time they would ever be together. 'God, what I wouldn't give . . .' She breaks it off then, away from what she's saying and to whom.

You jump right in there, a knight gallant. 'Well, you know what I'd want.'

'Oh yeah?' The comeback is snappy, sarcastic. 'You and every other horny driver in the joint.'

You push the point. 'How many times I propose to you anyway? Three?'

She laughs. Its starts out sarcastic but somehow ends up nostalgic. 'I think you left out a few. You were pretty loaded those last few times.'

You can't argue with that. 'Tell you what. You agree to marry me, I'll get you to Earth.'

'Yeah, sure.' The voice is firm but – there's hesitation.

'So it's a deal?'

She sucks in a breath. It's a whopper. When

60

she lets it out it comes with another whopper. 'John Canyon, you get me to Earth and if you still want to marry me I'll do it.'

You open your mouth but no words come out. You close it and open again. Words continue to remain stubbornly absent.

In the end she gives up waiting. 'I gotta get back to work.'

'Sure.' A moment, then more words than you thought you knew come, all of them in an inappropriate rush. 'Why don't we get together later, at your place. We could have a practice for when we're –'

She's already shaking her head. 'I ain't ready to dance to that tune again John. Not yet. Not with what I got on my mind.'

And with that she's gone, leaving you upset, vaguely unsatisfied and generally in need of either a drink or a fight.

Preferably both.

– 6 –

It's time to quit the ass end of the food chain and go looking for familiar faces. As it happens you find four at once, propping up a hullside table beside the row of observation windows lining one curved wall of the bar.

All four are drivers. Unfortunately their pristine Company whites give you a strange feeling in the pit of your stomach. There's something about being a walking advert for someone else's product that galls right down deep inside where you can never yank it out.

Still, they're the closest thing to mates you have on SkyTown. Finding them all here together in the bar is little more than a sign of the times: the Solar economy has entered its eighth year of recession. The Government has been promising for years that things are on the up, but as usual they're spouting more hot air than a damaged engine feed.

Jerry notices you first. He's tall, wiry, bald, nervous-looking. Who wouldn't be with job security as thin on the ground as it is? 'Hey, John.'

You mosey on over and take a seat.

'You still working independent?' That's Alex's way of saying 'Howdy'.

You nod. There's time to admit you're going on stony broke and this ain't it. 'Still own my own rig and pick my own loads.' You glance at the double helix logos stitched into the Company overalls. 'And I don't sell advertising space on my tits. If that's what you're talking about.'

A moment of silence, then Delia pops the question. 'You back for Kev's funeral?'

You shrug. 'Didn't hear. Which Kev? O'Brian? Or the red-headed Kev?'

There is another silence then. Tommy looks offended.

Jerry clarifies the matter. 'Kev the thief.'

Tommy looks real offended now.

'Well, he was.' Another silence, then Jerry continues, 'Took his load through the Scum Cluster trying to pick up time on a run. Not much of either came back out.'

You nod. 'Jackers.'

'And then some.'

'Word is Cap'n Macanudo stumbled on 'im.'

'Macanudo the Mako.'

'Guy's a damn depraved animal.'

'He's a devil.'

'Captured Kev and his load.'

'All they sent back was his dick.'

'They're using a matchbox as a coffin.'

Your eyes shift from one to the other as they speak. Their timing's slick as shit. You wonder how many times they've told this story. 'Poor Kev. Wasn't a bad guy, you overlook the stealing.'

Jerry adds, 'Anyways, we were planning on having a wake after the service. Think you might say a few words?'

You think about that one, but before you can respond, Tommy points out of the nearest observation window. 'Hey John, you hauling Interpork hogs?'

'They're my hogs till I get paid.' The response is automatic, as is the glance you send after Tommy's pointing finger. Disbelief is quickly replaced by anger. The windows have a perfect view out on to the mooring ring. The ring where *Betty* is docked. *Betty* but no trailers. The trailers are attached to the back of a cargo tug with an Interpork logo on the side. It's hauling them away.

'Do you see that? Do you? Some piece of garbage wrapped in human skin is jacking my load!'

And that's it. You've really seen red now. Forgetting about the familiar faces, or Kev's funeral, or the possibility of blagging a drink, you bolt for the entrance to the bar.

Keller is filling it.

You fetch up short, murder on your mind. You say nothing, however.

Keller's got a bailiff with him.

You wait.

Keller says with a smile, 'John Canyon, your load has been seized, square and legal.' He turns to the bailiff. 'Gimme those papers, Lou.'

Lou shakes his head. 'I like to serve 'em myself, Bix. Ain't proper otherwise.'

Keller sighs. 'It's important this gets done right. No – stylish. It's important this gets done stylish.' He takes the papers anyway and slaps them against your chest. It's all you can do to stop yourself ripping his arm off right here and now. Keller shoots a look at Lou. 'Hit him with the details.'

Lou says, formally, in a single breath, 'John Canyon your load has been seized by the Company pursuant to a court order appeals can be filed within thirty days at section forty-two superior court located on Ring Nine upside thank you for your time have a nice day.'

You blink. You wait another moment, aware of the growing interest in the proceedings by those eating at the bar. 'I don't need to wait two years to know I'm not getting paid a fair day's wage for a fair day's work.'

Lou says nothing but his expression makes his opinion clear. *I sure as hell don't get paid to sympathise with you, buddy. Haven't you heard? We're in a recession.*

You're about to respond when Keller jumps in again. 'You're blackballed with Interpork. You're blackballed with every division of the Company.' He smiles then. This moment is worth a fortune to him. 'I hear rumours of a load you ditched on Mars. I hear rumours of a dead man walking. I hear things, John, that a Company like HOKAI would be very interested to hear. So, if you yourself wish to remain in a condition to hear, see, think, and generally enjoy what piss-ant little life you have left, I suggest you get the hell off SkyTown and out of my sight.'

Another lingering grin and Keller is gone, Lou in tow.

When Cindy, oblivious to the proceedings having taken place while she was behind the bar, arrives with a plate of *hog a l'orange* on the house, you're so mad you can't even thank her.

Ass

– 1 –

Your name is Michael David Anghelides Pucci, you're at the controls of a Mammoth 3000 SuperTrucker. You're two light minutes from Saturn's rings and the flight instructor hasn't washed under his arms again today.

'Mister Pucci. When I tap the windscreen with my pencil, I want you to bring the vehicle to an emergency stop.'

It's the moment you've been waiting for the entire twenty-two years of your life.

The flight instructor clocks your grins and adds, 'A *controlled* emergency stop, Mister Pucci. *Controlled*. Is that clear?'

'Whatever. You got it. Just say the word.'

Twenty minutes later you're back at the station, clutching your pass certificate and heading for a cold beer while the flight instructor is still puking his guts up on the mooring ring.

The beer is interrupted by another call over the public address system.

You frown. What in the blue hell does Bix Keller want you for?

There's only one way to find out, and you take it. Keller's office is up on Ring Three, with a prime view of the hydrobays running down the station core. It's the only trees in a hundred AUs and you take every opportunity to rubberneck. The door to Keller's office opens and a secretary beckons you in. Keller himself is there, a grubby man at a grubby desk, fat and quivering in the down draft from an air conditioner mounted in the ceiling.

'You wanted to see me, Mister Keller?'

He nods, a quiver of jowls, a slippery look. You don't like this man. Problem is, he has power. Power and work. Both are at a premium out here.

'I understand you just graduated Space Truck school.'

You wave your certificate. 'Got it all right here. Got my temp medical and a class A permit –'

Keller shakes his head dismissively. 'Never mind that crap.' He thumbs through a well-thumbed ledger chained to his desk. 'Happens I need someone to push a consignment of square hogs to Oberon and Titania.'

A moment and your spine is crawling. You've got a bad feeling about this. 'Square hogs? Would that be John Canyon's load?'

Keller's screechy voice snaps like a broken piston rod. 'It's an *Interpork* load. I fired Canyon this morning.' He's sizing you up. You do your best to keep a poker face. He smiles. He knows what you're thinking anyway. 'You got a feeling about that one way or the other?'

You remember his tanned face, deep-set eyes. You remember the way he looked at Cindy, the way she looked at him. 'Not really, no.' You cringe inwardly. Why do you get the feeling you're selling Canyon out? You try to keep it straight for Keller and yourself. 'I barely know the guy.'

Keller nods, lightning quick; it takes the flesh of his face a second to catch up with the spasming muscles of his neck. 'Good. Because there's fifteen hundred out-of-work freight pushers here want this job.'

'Yeah, but I'm the best.' Only after you've said the words do you realise he was waiting for you to fill the gap.

'Your potential *is* frightening.' A long hard look. 'And I want Canyon to see just what it takes to replace him. Now. You want the job?'

You shrug. It's a tough world. 'Sure, I'll take it.'

'Good.' The ledger snaps shut with a businesslike clack. 'Pick up your pink probationary coveralls from Amos in Supply. See you keep 'em clean. When you're pink, you're Interport. Clear?'

You nod.

'Report back here at eighteen-hundred.'

That's it. It's over. Your first job. The moment you've been waiting for since you've been old enough to drive. You wonder why it's left you with such a peculiar feeling in your stomach. A feeling that you've just picked up something dirty and that it's stuck to you and gone all furry like a month-old Mars bar.

You decide a cold beer or three will wash away the bad taste in your mouth.

It doesn't.

The you remember the funeral.

– 2 –

You're Kev the Thief and if you were alive you'd be one cocky bastard and one lucky son-of-a-bitch. Problem for you is you're dead. That's pretty bad for you. Specially considering the way you clocked out: late on a load, using an illegal shortcut to make up the time, jacked, hacked, whacked and shot back in pieces via FedEx ballistic to your loved ones on SkyTown.

Your wife and kid on Earth aren't going to get a penny because you voided your insurance when you decided to run the Scum Cluster. Wendy will shed a few tears for you but she's young and pretty and just about to wise up to the world in a big way. She'll marry again quite soon and young Kevin will have a decent father and a decent shot at an education. Not that it'll do him any good in the long run – but then, hey, what are genes for, huh? See, there's a little bit of you left behind in your kid. A kind of genetic time-bomb named 'Kev' that will light up like a Christmas tree when little Kevin's pituitary gland kicks in about ten years from now. You ought to feel good about that.

Except of course you can't feel anything any more.

They bury you in the hydrobays. In space, everything is recyclable. You may have been a lousy asshole in life but the pieces of your body still contain essential chemical elements necessary for the pursuance of life for others in SkyTown.

You ought to be grateful really. It's your one and only shot at redemption and by God's great steel wheels they make sure you take it. A month from now and everyone you ever worked with'll be breathing you and drinking you and planting vegetables and vat yeast in you.

Kinda moving, ain't it?

All your friends think so, anyways. They're all here: Jerry, Delia, Tommy, Alex, Cindy, Pucci. Even John Canyon's here, with an expression that says, *not another damn funeral*. Hundreds of others are watching from the offices surrounding the core. Well, they glance up from

71

their work every now and then just long enough to wonder what the little bunch of people is doing here in the fresh air and artificial rain when they could be earning a living instead.

The service doesn't take long, then it's back to the bar for them and back to the food chain for you.

Better luck next life.

– 3 –

Back in the Space-Ring Burger Bar conversation is as predictable as the results of a faulty after-burner on liftoff.

'– use a beer, I could really –'

'– goddamn jackers comes after us company people like –'

'– heard the Company was gonna hunt them down but –'

'– sent some major Bear into the Scum Cluster last –'

'– two gunships and neither of 'em came –'

'– you notice how quiet they kept that? –'

You listen to the conversation, but don't really take it in. It kinda slides over your head like the rain at the funeral. The funeral. Something about the funeral –

No.

The hydrobays. Something about the hydrobays.

Yeah.

For a while there you were back on Earth. Back on the place where you were born. The only place in the system with blue skies and tall grass and genuine smiles you don't have to look at through breather masks and where the air don't melt your lungs and the seas won't freeze you into a carbon-flavoured popsicle.

'Course you could be fantasising all that. It has been quite a while. Like thirty-eight years to be exact. Thirty-nine counting that half a year spent on Mars.

Jesus. Thirty-nine years. That's more'n twice as long as Cindy is old.

Jesus God and his great steel wheels.

Time for a rest.

Maybe time to hang up the old iron, quit the spacelanes.

Maybe.

You shrug, grab a beer, slug it down in one, grab another. Each beer simplifies the problem.

Quit the road?

You're John Canyon and, on balance, you'd rather quit breathing.

You take a break between beers, become aware someone's calling your name. It's Delia. 'You gonna make that speech, John? Someone's got to say something.'

You shrug, take another slug of beer. 'I'm kinda drawing a blank.'

Delia hands you another beer. 'Yeah? Have another one. Didn't you work with Kev back in the old days? Hauling hydrospares outta the lunar well?'

You ponder that long enough for Alex to step in with a few choice words.

'He did work alongside us for eight years. I remember he found my keys once. I'd dropped 'em in the urinal when I was pissed. Leastways that's what he said.' A pause for hiccups, then, 'You know, I always wondered what he was doing when he found them keys. Guess I'll never –' a burp '– never know, right?'

You blink. That was heavy.

Jerry adds, 'Maybe his sense of humour wasn't so great – and nobody said Kev was a perfect human being, but he's gone now, forever, and we owe him the respect of a few short words, that's all.' Jerry looks at you. 'Someone's gotta do it.'

Delia chips in. 'If he'd lived longer, he might have become a better person, you know . . .'

Someone takes your arm. You don't need to look. You practically memorised her body heat last time. Cindy says, 'Come on John, you're the oldest here. They respect you. They're looking to you.'

You look at her then.

And you do it.

You climb on to the bar and stand there, a beer

74

in each hand, eyes filled with Company whites breathing adspace, and independents, and one proby pink named Puccini or Pachelbel or something like that, which really ought to mean something but in the heat of the moment seems to be lost.

You begin to speak. 'I've been –'

You realise no-one is listening. You wait for quiet then begin again. 'I've been asked to say a few words on behalf of the late Kev the – I mean, Kevin Sanderson senior.'

The crowd go wild. Well, they mutter between beers for you to get on with it.

'Ah. You see. It's like this.'

Try as you might, not one thing about Kevin Sanderson senior comes to mind. Not his hair colour, his religious persuasion or even his favourite drink. Either the alcohol has eradicated it forever from accessible memory or you really never did know the guy.

'See . . . Kev, he was . . . Well, I knew his brother. Sean. His brother Sean. And . . . his brother Sean . . .'

Its' time to get down before you fall down.

' . . . he was worse.'

Silence.

'Thank you.'

You manage to get off the bar by swinging momentarily from the neon Saturn-and-onion-ring logo, and head for the door. Half-pissed Space Truckers offer solemn handshakes as you go. A mood of grim fraternity has taken hold of the normally cheerful bar.

Cindy wanders up then, tries to lighten the mood. 'Hey, John. Mike passed his test. Got himself a job.'

'Mike? Oh, Mister Pink, you mean?' Cindy looks taken aback at the venom in your voice. Well, hell, let her be taken aback. The significance of the pink proby had finally sunk in – and you're getting mad. You look around for the pinks. They're not hard to spot. 'Well, looky here. A new man and a new load. Normally we'd have some kinda blow-out for that. But I see from your pyjamas who you're working for. Which is nothing to celebrate.'

Cindy's hand is on your arm. 'John, not everybody's got their own rig. Not everyone can afford to work independent.'

And then he's there in your face. Pink and earnest. Respect oozing out of every pore like the smell of the night-before's curry. 'Hey, John. I'm sorry 'bout you losing your load but this was my only shot. I'm outta cash, outta credit and someone has to get those hogs to Oberon and Titania.'

Somehow the lad's earnest apology only seems to make you angrier. 'You took a fearless moral inventory kid, and then you took my job. If you can live with that, fine. I don't have to. Hump yourself down to the other end of the bar 'fore I plant ya beside ol' Kev out in the hydrobays.'

Give him his due, Mister Pink rises indignantly to the occasion. 'Now I treat you with respect, don't I? All I ask is that you do the same –'

His words slide past unnoticed. What you've noticed instead is Keller and his girls filling the entrance to the bar. They've got *fuck you, Canyon* written all over them.

'Hey, kid, your boss has brought the circus with him.'

You are pleased to note that Jackie is wearing a number of electrical burns along his left hand and arm. Proof, if any were needed, that they didn't get away with your load entirely unscathed. There's a fleeting moment when you wish you'd set *Betty*'s cattleprod to high. Ah well. There'll be other times. Like now for example, by the look of it.

Keller takes a step forward. Mel and Jackie follow in perfect sync. 'We've come to pay our respects.'

The hell with this bullshit. 'Circus? Trained turds more like.'

Jackie moves towards you. You match him step for step, glare for glare. You smile at Jackie. 'Want to be careful around my rig, sonny. *Betty*

77

bites.' You nod to the burns on Jackie's arm. Jackie snarls.

Delia tries to cool things off. She mumbles something but Keller's having none of it. This is his time and everyone's going to know about it. 'Slam your teeth, Delia.'

She does.

'I want you off SkyTown, Canyon.'

You say nothing. You are watching the girls. They're the dangerous ones.

'You hearing me, Canyon?' Keller's voice is an irritating bleat.

'I'd like to oblige you. If you'd paid me I'd be gone by now.'

Keller's voice takes on a self-righteous whine. 'We fuelled your rig. Even though the damn thing nearly killed my boy here. Cattleprods are illegal, Canyon, in case you didn't know. You're lucky Jackie here's decided not to press charges.'

You laugh. 'I'm surprised both your boys between 'em have got the wit to decide anything, Keller.'

That one drew a sigh from the onlookers. Score one for John Canyon. Like it's gonna do you any good.

Keller scowls. 'Move your ass down to the mooring ring, get in your rig and get off this station. Do it now and you won't get hurt.'

Something goes off in your head then, a little

skyrocket of pure anger. Buzzed with adrenalin and more than half pissed, you move like chain lightning. 'Like this, you mean?'

Before Keller can move, your fist is buried in his stomach. All the air goes out in a big gasp and he's sitting on the floor in a puddle of upturned food.

The girls move in then, expressions slowly changing to delight as they realise you've given them the excuse they need to finish the fight. Well, hell, let 'em try it.

They do.

You get in two good punches. You black Mel's eye and break another of Jackie's teeth. Boy, that lad will never learn to keep his chin down.

Problem is by then Keller's up and it's three on one.

The end is inevitable.

A punch loops out of nowhere and it all goes black for a bit. When the lights come back on Jackie and Mel have hold of you and Keller's hitting you in all the soft places.

Behind Keller you get the vague impression of movement. Of a protest by someone in pink. The blows stop for a bit. Keller turns. 'What? Somebody say something? Come on now, any of you space dropouts want to make something of it? Well, butt the fuck out then?'

And then he's looking at you again. He's a bit

red in the face by now, though that's probably got more to do with the trickle of blood running into your eye than it has any effort on his part.

'You don't mess with me, Canyon. And you never, ever, mess with the Company.'

He winds up for another punch. Someone grabs his arm. Someone pink. Puccini, bless his stupid name.

'Now hold on, Mister Keller. This man's within his rights here –'

'Let go my arm, kid, or by God's great steel wheels you'll find out what it's like to breathe vacuum too.'

Prophetic words, as it turns out.

Instead of letting go, Mike lands a punch that has Keller reeling.

Using the distraction, you manage to pull free of the girls long enough to butt Keller savagely in the face as he reels past. The fat man's nose crunches and blood explodes across his face. His voice is an indignant squeal.

'Keep away from me, Canyon! Mel! Jackie! What the hell'm I payin' ya for? Do something!'

The next few moments are over fast, far too fast – it's difficult to remember which order things happen in. But you remember how it starts.

It starts when Mel pulls his gun.

The gun is aimed square at your back when

Cindy smashes it aside with a scalding pot of coffee. Mel screams, the gun fires wild and one of the narrow observation ports lining the bar's outside wall explodes in a spray of glass. Immediately a new scream replaces Mel's: the scream of atmosphere draining out into space. The air is full of loose trash, some of it human. Food, crockery, caps, drinks, even someone's shoe are all sucked out into the big dark. Alarms wail and somewhere back of the bar pressure doors are sliding shut, contributing towards the mass exodus from the section.

Keller's voice jacks up above the general hubbub in a panicky screech as he is sucked through the air towards the window.

Twenty years ago you heard the dying scream of a cloud miner trapped in Jupiter's gravity well. It's stayed with you this long. Only Keller's scream beats it for sheer pathetic desperation.

The scream lengthens, then, surprisingly, turns into the wet thump of flesh against metal. There is a moment of quiet filled only with a few astonished yelps and a moan of pain.

Keller has stumbled against the window and is now blocking it. The coaming is about six inches smaller than his ass, which is sealed against it tighter than a jam-tin lid.

He blinks. His face moves in slow comprehension. First surprise at finding himself alive, then growing alarm as his backside begins to make movements and noises entirely without his volition and, finally, pain as he feels several jagged bits of glass still attached to the port coaming grind into his ass.

'Help! Somebody help me!'

With Keller blocking the port the alarms shut down and the pressure doors roll open. You take a moment to think about how smart the computers on SkyTown are. Then there is a ripping noise and Keller screams. His scream is loud and long. Blood erupts around the waistband of his trousers.

He jerks backwards into the port. Just a couple of inches. Enough to give a taster of what is to come.

By now his yells for help have dissolved into pain-filled squeals. His body jerks again. He is folded almost double. You can hear a strained ripping sound. You hope it's only his clothes.

Everyone in the bar is motionless, staring at Keller, folded in half into the port. As one, half a dozen people conquer their surprise, run forward to help. It's too late.

A moment of time, a final despairing cry, and you are treated to the terrible and fascinating sight of a twenty-two-stone man being sucked ass-first through a ten-inch porthole.

Keller gone, the airscream jacks itself up to ear-splitting intensity, more loose trash follows the big man into the big dark. The alarms come back on and the pressure doors are rolling shut again.

Grabbing Cindy, you make for the nearest door. It slams shut in your face. The bar's empty by now. Everyone safe except Mel and Jackie who, stupidly trying to help their boss, had been caught too close to the port. They are flopping about in the rush of air, coughing blood and gurgling for help you cannot give.

By now your skin is prickling with decompression blisters. The last safety door is trolling shut about twenty feet away. Someone's there, trying to hold it open. Someone pink.

With all your strength you throw Cindy towards the kid. He catches her and shoves her through the fast-closing hatch. You fight for breath. You fight against the airstream. Your legs are killing you. You begin to get an idea of the panic and fear that old cloud miner felt as he was sucked beyond help down into Jupiter's gravity well.

'Goddamn kid, you're gonna blow out the entire section if that door ain't shut!'

The kid's voice is a thin scream in the depressurising bar. '*Just get your ass through here now, Canyon, and quit yapping!*'

It's surprise as much as fear that gets you through the hatch.

83

It seals shut behind you with a reassuring solid thump, taking the heel of your left spaceboot with it.

You take a moment to get your breath back. Alarms are still mouthing off, right across the ring. Confused and frightened voices are raised in a football-crowd babble. The measured thump of Marshall Mbotumi's men can be heard approaching fast.

They'll want the man who started the fight. You know what they'll do when they catch you.

The kid knows too. 'Jesus Christ Almighty, what are we gonna do? They catch you, man, they'll space you!'

You answer the kid's question by grabbing him and Cindy and dragging them both into the nearest ladies' excuse-me.

Inside the rest-room you hunker down on to your hands and knees and scoot along the tiled floor. Peripherally you are aware that Cindy and the kid are staring at you as if you're raving mad. Hell, maybe you are.

The kid's babbling, 'Wrong door, man, wrong door –'

You tell him to shut it. His mouth, that is. Underneath the door of the last stall you see a pair of feet. The feet are wrapped in a pair of coveralls and are quite still. Far too still for someone who has just crapped their way through a major atmosphere blowout.

You stand up, wrench open the stall door.

The kid is blathering incoherently now. He must really think you've lost it. Cindy is saying nothing, bless her. She always knows when to cut and when to run.

The stall is occupied by a plump woman somewhere in her sixties. Sparing no thought at all for what someone of that apparent age would be doing in SkyTown, you move forward.

Her eyes widen. 'Get out! What are you doing? Get out! Occupied! Get out! I'll scream for the Marshall, you filthy man! Get –'

That's enough of that. You reach into her mouth and pull open the top of her face. Immediately her voice becomes muffled. Inside her face is a clear plastic flipcatch covering a button. You throw the catch to expose the button and beckon the others into the stall.

Eyes wide, both Cindy and the kid comply.

You slam the door just as the outside door opens to admit a flood of SkyTown deputies. The kid opens his mouth to squeak – a protest or a question. Whichever, you silence him with a gesture.

You push the button, then quickly flip the woman's face shut again. The floor of the stall, minus toilet and mumbling woman, descends quickly.

You're in an elevator.

You drop past the woman's face, her hips, her ankles and their wrappings. The toilet bowl glides silently upwards. The ceiling slides into place to form a new floor above, just as the deputies open the stall door. You hear the woman protest loudly, and the embarrassed deputies back apologetically from the stall.

Then all sounds from above fade into the gurgling of plumbing and the rattle of deeply buried atmosphere recyclers. You're going underground, in more ways than one.

The kid looks like he's going to ask more questions. You shut him down fast with a look and a word. He's unhappy but goes along for the ride. You take a quick glance at Cindy. She's with you, no fuss, just watching everything. Smart girl.

The elevator stops and the door opens. You step out. It's dark and damp and smelling.

SkyTown isn't a normal city. It wasn't built on a river and it doesn't have sewers. It has its own equivalent though. A waste-reclamation system which threads its way through the bowels of the space-city in ways even its builders have forgotten. There's free water here, lichen, mould, vermin – rats and spiders and the like carried in on ships from groundports.

Not all the vermin are animals.

It's one of these human gutter-rats that you want to see now.

His name is Zesty. He's your basic black-mar-keteer, scum-of-the-earth freeloader. He doesn't pay tax and he has been known to kill people who've tried to collect it from him. On Mars it was Zesty who made it possible for you to die. His agents supplied the damaged suit and a corpse grown from your DNA. He facilitated your illegal change of name and ident number, put you on to the load of Interpork hogs and arranged for your bribe to reach the freighter despatcher in Hogtown Skyport.

In this whole filthy, garbage-ridden system he's about your only real friend.

If anyone can help you now, he can.

All you have to do is find him before Marshall Mbotumi and his deputies find you.

As it turns out, finding Zesty is a lot easier than you expected.

You realise that when you walk into the guns, and the efficient, rather dour men and women pointing them at you.

– 4 –

You call Zesty by a man's name but really that is a convenience for you. In reality Zesty is of inde-terminate sex, and so old it begs the question. His frame is huge and strangely sculpted; a lifetime spent in gravity other than Earth's will do that to a man. His clothes hold an oily sheen. He sits at a desk in a cathedral of waste-pipes. The desk is huge, iron-black and oil-sheened, with lichen lamps growing along the front and sides. The desk is full of objects almost as strange as Zesty himself. Many of them are old and made of wood. Some are well preserved, some are rotting. You have heard rumours that one or two of them originated inside the Great Pyramid of Cheops, but that may be a vanity on Zesty's part. Things move sluggishly on the top and sides of the desk. Things that aren't part of Zesty. Or perhaps they are.

In the middle of this cornucopia of strangeness two islands of familiarity blink: laser specs bio-welded to Zesty's cheeks. Now your eyes adjust to the gloom you make out more details: the specs project infobeams directly on to Zesty's retinas. His eyelids have been removed. Voluntarily he allows himself no respite from the rivers of information datastreamed along the hundreds of conduits which fall in jungle loops from the ceiling and walls of his grotto and attach to his desk.

His voice is a tiny whisper amongst all this greatness.

'Give me one good reason why I shouldn't kill you now.'

With Zesty there's always a question. 'I killed your wife for you, didn't I?'

A thoughtful pause. Machinery – or is it claws? – ticks quietly in the darkness.

'A good enough reason.'

You try not to let him hear your sigh of relief. Dealing with Zesty is a chance happening at best.

'This wouldn't be strictly a social call, would it, John?'

You consider the question. Actually there's not much to consider. 'I need to get off the hub. I need a load.'

A sigh in the darkness.

'You need another favour?'

The kid opens his great trap and starts in with some macho bullshit. You kick him fast and he shuts it just as fast.

Cindy is still mute like she was born that way.

''Sright.' You emphasise the point. 'I need a favour.'

'I see three of you here, am I right, John? Three of you and one favour? You see the implied contradiction?'

The kid loses it then. 'We're partners. This old-timer has lost me one load already. If you got a load for him it's for me too.'

You sigh. Cindy says nothing. Not with her mouth anyways.

Zesty makes a sound like wind in trees. You

can tell from his reaction that the kid finds it scary. Never heard it before, see. It's Zesty's *I'm interested* sound. It's his *tell me more* sound.

The last time you heard that sound was three hours before you died.

Cindy opens her mouth then and adds one word that flips the equation on its head. 'Please.'

A movement. You have never heard of Zesty moving. Certainly he has no need of movement. But he moves now. He looks at Cindy.

She doesn't flinch.

The moss-light from the desk brightens until she is outlined in a dreadful glow. Fortunately, growing from the front of the desk, the moss-light hides rather than reveals details of Zesty's body.

Still Cindy doesn't move.

At the edges of the chamber metallic noises echo as concealed men and women arm hidden weapons. You can bet they've thought about atmosphere blowouts down here too. If Zesty takes it into his head that Cindy was being cheeky . . .

But he doesn't.

His voice is still a sigh, but the tone is different. You have never heard it like this. 'An appeal to my sentimental side.' Something creaks. Skin slithers across his face until he is smiling. From somewhere in the depths of the grotto comes a startled gasp, quickly cut off.

Zesty continues. 'I shall open my heart at once. I do have something. Something unpleasant, I fear.'

The kid says, 'We'll take it.'

You frown. 'You're a passenger, not a partner.' You look back towards Zesty. 'I can't pay you.'

'Killing my wife counts only for so much credit.'

Shit. He wants to deal.

'However, you paid cash for our previous transaction. And we are –' a sigh '– friends.' A moment to let the echoes of his voice fade. 'You can have this one on the house, John.'

Oh shit, it's worse than you thought.

'What've you got?' The kid again, damn his mouth, and suddenly the option to refuse is gone.

The desk chatters brightly to itself. Something creeps along the surface. Rats? A snake? Some piece of Zesty?

It's a printout. The kid grabs it. 'Rush shipment to Earth. Two-day schedule. Thirty-eight trailers to be left in high orbit on arrival.'

'Earth.' It's Cindy. Her voice glows with hope. Shit, now they've all been suckered.

You give in to the inevitable. 'We'll do it. What's the cargo?'

The kid shuffles the damp manifest. 'Extruded polymer sexual surrogates.'

Cindy grins.

And why not? Wouldn't you grin if you knew the load responsible for getting you half-way across the Solar System was thirty-eight trailers full of sex dolls?

You become aware that Zesty is looking at Cindy again. He knows she wants to go to Earth. He knows everything. You'd bet your Auntie Hettie's microwave he knows what's in those trailers.

And you'd bet your life it ain't sex dolls.

As it happens your life is exactly the stake on the table; yours, Cindy's, the kid's; a considerable portion of human life on Earth, for that matter.

You just don't know it yet.

Bear

– 1 –

You can hear something. Something beyond the dripping of the pipes, the soft pulse of Zesty's breathing and the scuttle of rats. Something you shouldn't be hearing. Not yet. You look around. Everyone else can hear it too.

A cry of indignation, quickly muted; the flush of a ladies' excuse-me. A moment, then footsteps. Lots of footsteps: clunking, confident, arrogant footsteps. The clinking of guns.

Soft-projectile guns. Hull-friendly guns.

Marshall's guns.

'They've found us.'

You don't need him to tell you that; you are already diving flat in the muck to avoid the bullets.

The crossfire gets real bad for a while as Zesty's protection takes on the Marshall's hired guns.

You roll around, manage to find Cindy, grab her hand, drag her clear of the fighting.

'You OK?'

'Yeah.'

The kid creeps up then, amazement and sewer muck plastered in an uneasy mixture on his face. 'They didn't ask anyone to surrender. They just opened fire.'

'Yeah, well, what do you suppose they have to lose? The lives of a bunch of sewer rats who are messing up the economy anyway?'

'Jeez Louise.'

The firing stops.

You hear the sound of running feet, shouts, swearing. Lots of swearing. There are more shots, single ones, the sound of things falling, other sounds as of things being dragged away.

After a while everything goes quiet.

It stays quiet for a long while.

Eventually you peer out of the little side tunnel in which you've been hiding.

No Marshall. No deputies.

Nothing.

Zesty has vanished. So has his desk, his protection, every trace he was ever here. There's no blood, no bodies, no spent ammo, no dropped weapons.

Nothing.

'Man, the rats down here are bad-asses.'

Ignoring the kid, you lead the way into a nearby tunnel. It's time to put as much distance between you and trouble as humanly possible. You slosh through the muck as quietly as you can.

Five minutes goes by. Ten minutes.

Nothing.

Fifteen minutes.

Still nothing.

You're just starting to think you've made it into the clear when you hear running footsteps coming after you down the tunnel.

'Shit.'

Torch light glimmers on the tunnel wall. Rats skitter out from underfoot.

'Double shit with nuts and wafers.'

Cindy and the kid are already running.

The kid whispers urgently: 'Haul it, Canyon. They find us here they're gonna space our asses.'

He's not wrong.

'Kid?'

'Yeah?'

'Gimme that cargo manifest.'

His look tells you to stop wasting time. You toss the look right back at him, grab the manifest and then hit them with the nasty bit.

'We're gonna have to split up. *Bitchin' Betty*'s docked at the mooring ring, low-side. Can't miss her, she's the only rig with no cargo. Be there in an hour. We unhook in one hour ten.'

The kid hesitates, stares at the cargo manifest. 'Partners?'

'Passengers.'

'How do we know we can trust you?'

95

'Ten seconds from now this place is gonna be a zoo and then it's all over anyway. Now go on – get.'

You grab Cindy's arm and try to drag her off. She won't be dragged. You persist. She glares at you and takes off into the tunnels on her own.

'Not that way! Jeez, kid, will you –'

You stop. The kid has already gone.

The footsteps are closing in.

You run.

– 2 –

The only thing going for you is that the Marshall and his deputies don't know who you are. That is, they obviously know they're looking for someone – and that someone made his escape into the sewers. But who that someone is would be arguable at the best of times. There are three important facts on your side. One: they don't know how many were sucked into space – or who they were. Two: they don't know how many people they killed in the sewers – or who they were. And three: the only guys who would rat you out are currently doing the human equivalent of baked Alaska somewhere out in the big dark.

This is good; it means you stand a reasonable chance of getting away from SkyTown – assuming you can make it back to *Betty* in one piece.

The problem is: you aren't as young as you used to be, not by a long chalk. That's going to make the going hard. Still, you've got your freedom and future profit clutched in your hand in the shape of Zesty's cargo manifest – and that keeps those cute little legs of yours pumping through the muck-and-glummery of the SkyTown sewer system.

In fact it keeps them pumping long enough to lose the bear, lose yourself amongst the SkyTown trash and find yourself again, conveniently, in the atmosphere ducting which services the mooring ring.

Less than thirty minutes after Keller spilled his guts ass-first into the big dark you're safe in *Bitchin' Betty*, cattleprod set, warming up the systems and planning your escape route from SkyTown.

First of all, though, there's the cargo to pick up. According to the manifest, it's waiting for you in the loading dock, an anonymous daisy chain of trailers, one of many destined for distant ports.

The cattleprod sparks and there's a screech from *Betty*'s passenger lock.

It's the kid. His hands are scorched where he reached for the door controls. He's fuming. You're too busy laughing to care. You grab a squeeze-tube of Germolene from the medical box and toss it to him. He fumbles the catch and has to chase the tube around the 'pit.

Then you realise: Cindy's not with him.

The kid stares at the open floor hatch and beyond it, to *Betty*'s guts lying exposed, then up to the wrench in your hand. 'This gonna take long? There's troopers all over the place.'

You shake your head. 'You see Cindy? You see her coming?'

He registers the concern in your voice. 'No. You think the Marshall got her?'

'No reason why he should. She didn't do anything, now did she?'

'Like knock the guy's gun away so he shot out the window and killed three guys, including himself, you mean?'

You shake your head, dive back into the floor hatchway. 'She'll make it. Gimme that other wrench willya?'

The kid obliges; the handle of the wrench is liberally smeared with Germolene. 'Hey – you know you've got mustard all over your thruster touchscreen?'

You wipe the wrench on your coveralls and use it to point to the vacant space next to Aunt Hettie's microwave where there are attachments for a refrigerator, but no unit. 'I don't buy extras, kid.'

'So you use your dashboard as a cupboard?'

'Look, change the subject willya, kid?'

He shrugs. 'Sure.' A pause. You can almost hear the gears clashing inside his head. 'I like Cindy. She's OK.'

You sigh. 'She's got a kind nature and she's trying to be hospitable.' *Who are you trying to kid? The kid is eye-candy and she's got an appetite.* 'She's got other things on her mind.'

The kid grins. 'Let's just say I'm grateful she's making the effort to be kind, then.' He peers down the hatchway after you. You feel him hovering there, trying to make you feel he could be useful. You're not fooled. 'So . . . in the light of that . . . you mind if I ask you what the deal is with you and Cindy, John?'

You feign ignorance. 'Don't get you.'

'Well. I think she likes me and I'd like to pursue it further. So . . . you know . . . I'd like to know if you're involved.'

Involved?!

You fix the last doodad, jump up into the 'pit, slam and bolt the hatch. 'Kid, a gentleman never answers a question like that.'

'So that's a "no" then.'

You're about to explain it to him when the hatch pops open and Cindy charges in. She's changed her clothes, showered, applied some make-up and a dab of perfume. Subtle. You just managed to get here without a belly full of bullet holes and she managed to do all that.

'Sorry I'm late. I had to give Habib thirty seconds' notice. Grab some clothes, you know, Girl stuff.'

You shake your head admiringly. 'Girl stuff.'

'You have a problem with that?'

'Absolutely not.'

She hands you the case for stowing. As she does so a catch pops and some stuff slips out. It floats around the 'pit until you and the kid retrieve it. The kid ends up with her underwear, you end up with a solid photo. A beautiful woman; a twin to Cindy right down to the gypsy eyes and hair.

'It's my mother, Carol.' She reaches for the solid but you hang on to it. 'It was taken before I was born.' A moment. 'Before she got ill.'

You are mesmerised by the image. 'Carol . . .' You blink. You feel like something has come loose inside. Irritably you shake off the feeling. 'I see where you get your looks. I woulda liked to have met her back then.'

Cindy shoots you a funny look. Curiosity? Amusement? Sympathy? Jealousy? Suddenly your head's pounding and you don't know where to look. You turn away and the kid's there with the empty squeeze-tube of Germolene and a pertinent observation.

'Hadn't we better get the hell outta here?'

Cindy takes the solid from you and stuffs it

back into the case.

You show her how to collar into *Betty*'s passenger seat. The kid you let fend for himself.

You tell *Betty* to uncouple the docking collar and fire up the manoeuvring thrusters.

You've got a cargo to collect.

– 3 –

It's waiting for you in the loading ring, exactly where Zesty said it would be, cradled in the arms of the final assembly plant. There are thirty-seven trailers and every one looks like it's already come a long way. The trailers are matt black, pitted and scarred by space junk, paint peeling. They look like they've come on a fast train out of hell. They give you a bilious feeling like mild food-poisoning. You can't help thinking of Zesty's last words: *You can have this load on the house*.

It doesn't help your digestion.

You tell *Betty* to perform a slow transit. You want to get a good look at these babies before tying on.

Betty does as she's told. The laterals kick and you're sliding sideways along the loading bay, parallel to the trailers, past rigs and cargo cranes and suited dock workers – all of whom, you notice, seem to be taking great pains to stay as far from your load as possible.

And there's another weird thing about these

trailers. Cindy notices it. 'They've got no logos. No Company insignia. Everything's made by someone. Why not advertise?'

The kid tries to lighten the mood. 'Yeah, well, if you were hauling twenty-five thousand sex dolls half way across creation would you want to shout about it?'

Cindy shrugs. You wonder if she feels as creeped out about this whole deal as you do.

You voice your fear. 'I don't know what's in them trailers. But I bet you a billion-dollar refit to a bent dime it ain't no sex dolls.'

They're looking at you now. Something in your voice tells them what's chugging through your head.

The kid spots it first. 'You want to ditch this load? Get another job?'

There's no option and you know it. 'Where we gonna get another job now? Besides – what about Cindy? She needs to get to Earth, right?'

She nods. She knows what you're thinking. Space is big. Space is dark. And sure as your mother slapped you for swiping the cookie jar, there ain't no-one in space'll help you if a load ain't what it ought to be.

'Course by the time you find out it's generally too late. You tell them about Droogie Dupont. 'Company Security caught Droogie cracking Earth-orbit with fifty trailers of spare parts.

Live organs. Human organs, you get my drift? Several kinds of immoral and illegal. Droogie didn't know. The cargo manifest said he was hauling ten thousand tins of Alphabetti Spaghetti. Thing is, his signature was on it. That was a decade since. I hear he might be out of jail next fall on good behaviour – if he's really lucky.'

'Jeez.' The kid is impressed. Even Cindy's eyes are wide – and she's heard the story before.

'Is my point coming across here?'

The kid nods soberly. 'That we don't really know what we're getting into? Yeah?'

Cindy adds, 'That we don't know what's in them trailers? Sure.'

You cap it off with, 'And if we don't have a choice? Yeah, we know that alright. *Bitchin' Betty*, I want you to tie on to those trailers and prepare to leave the ring.'

Betty does as she's told. There are three solid lurches as the docking collar attaches and the locking clamps snuggle home. Then there are three more solid lurches.

'The hell was that?'

'*Betty*, kick in the rearview, willya? Show me the towbars.'

Betty obliges. Three thick metal clamps have closed over the towbars. 'Where'n the blue hell did they come from?'

Betty tells you she has no idea where the extra metal came from.

Cindy is peering closely at the rearview screen. 'They came outta the trailers.'

The kid's all over her. 'How did you know that?'

She gives him a look that would fry platinum. 'I got eyes, don't I? You can see the hatch coamings.'

She's right.

'Where's that manifest? It never said nothing about no darn cargo clamps!'

'Well, how do we get them off?'

'I don't know!' You feel sick. You feel like something real nasty's got a hold of both you and *Betty* and ain't planning on letting go until the last trump. 'Goddamn Zesty, goddamn manifest, goddamn favours! Goddamn I wish I'd never killed his goddamn wife!' Blustering helps, but only for a moment. You're not normally given to bluster. It's having passengers. That's what's doing it. Having passengers in the rig. You should be alone. Just you and *Betty*.

'Hey John . . .' Cindy's eyes are wide, interested. 'Did you really kill that guy Zesty's wife?'

Something tells you this trip's going to be hell on wheels.

You are saved from answering when the

assembly plant gives you the green light and releases the trailers. Or maybe the trailers release the plant.

You shove forward on the stick and *Betty* eases forward.

The trailers come with you.

The loading ring glides slowly past. Rigs, trailers, cranes, dockers, cargo pods, concession stalls. They're all getting out of your way now. And the radio traffic is ignoring you. It's like you're invisible; like once you tied on to those trailers you became one with whatever is inside them. Whatever they all *think* is inside them.

You slide out of the ring and kick in the main thrusters. Two minutes later you're in an exit vector and SkyTown is falling behind in the rearview.

You're half way through telling *Betty* to calculate a high-orbital solution on Earth-space when the shadow of a Transport Trooper Mobile Unit – *bear* to you – falls across the windscreen and a scratchy, self-important voice crackles out of the radio and tells you you're under arrest.

– 4 –

You swear. You've had it with these dumb schmucks. They've jacked your load, withheld your pay, nearly killed you on numerous occasions. And they're supposed to be the good guys.

You switch off the radio in mid-squawk and slam the pedal to the metal.

Betty leaps like she's been kicked. The hull creaks, the trailers rattle, and then you're moving away from SkyTown at high-g.

The bear stays with you. He's joined by three others. *Betty* tells you about it, relaying radar info in a slightly panicky voice.

Cindy says nothing and this time the kid joins in. Maybe some of her good sense is rubbing off on him.

Whatever. You can worry about that later.

For now there's just the adrenalin bashing through your body, the buzz in your head that says you've got a terminal case of go-fast fever.

You tap the brakes, stamp on the go-juice. Up ahead a tethered neon reads:

Castlemaine XXXX
Australians wouldn't give a XXXX
for any other lager.

Betty takes out the hoarding, mooring lines, anchor and all. Debris slashes past the windscreen, crackling with uncontrolled energy.

Four bears are right up your ass, the whole

way – four troop-carriers; and a baby two-seater hiding behind the sign makes five.

Goddamn bears – thicker'n bugs on a bumper these days.

You're in SkyTown's approach vector now, going the wrong way – and there's a rig heading straight for you. Another goddamn Mammoth. The radio's off so you can only imagine the freight-driver's startled blasphemy. You tell *Betty* to hold her course. The Mammoth swerves, jack-knifing and spilling its load: twenty-some trailers on a direct collision course. You wrench the stick and manage to avoid the leaders.

The trailers tumble past. One collides with a police cruiser. One bear out of the race. The rest are shot to dust by the other bears' meteorite defence systems.

Saying a quick prayer for the unknown trucker's insurance paperwork, you stamp on the gas. Two seconds later you're heading out of SkyTown space on an oblique vector, a posse of bear on your bumper and a grin plastered across your face that says *kick ass*.

The radio crackles. You don't want to talk to bear so you kick it off. They stay with you, too dumb to give up.

By now Saturn is swelling above the dash. It's pink and brown and swirly, bisected by the glittering edge of the ring system. Two hundred thousand miles of cold ice.

Ho ho ho children. It's time to go sledgin'.

You yank the stick and kick in the afterburners, scraping aside congealed mustard to do so. The rings stretch right across the windscreen. *Betty* skitters towards them like an excited puppy let off the leash for the first time in a month.

The kid is making strangled noises. 'You trying to say somethin', kid? 'Cause if y'are, speak up: I kinda got my hands full here, if y'catch my drift.'

The kid chokes a singles word: 'Rings.'

You grin.

'What're you worried about, kid? You did this on your test, am I right? Took the Cassini division at point oh-six cee and parked nose-on to Shepherd Moon B and had a prime instructor puking his guts up, am I right?'

The kid squeaks. 'That was in a goddamn Mammoth! I had computer-assisted steering!'

'Well, we got *Betty* don't we?'

'*Betty*'s a goddamn *Pachyderm*!'

'Now don't let me hear you talk that way about my second best girl, you hear? Have a little faith – keep your eyes open. You might learn something.'

'I learned something already, Canyon, and that's that you're a raving lunatic who don't deserve to draw breath, let alone marry a pretty girl like Cindy.'

You shoot them a sideways glance – and grin. Cindy looks like she'd brain the kid if she only dared unlock the safety collar on her seat. 'Take it from me, kid, you're gonna regret that. Meantime, buckle up and button up! I gotta concentrate.'

The rings swell from a line to a band, to a thick swathe across the windscreen. Jagged lumps of rock and ice backlit by the swollen gas giant whose gravity had captured them so long ago.

The sound of that old forty-niner's squeal as he dropped into Jupiter's gravity well pounds in your head like old blood.

It's joined by the rattle of dust against the hull.

Cindy's eyes narrow.

'Don't sweat it, babe. *Betty* charge the hull. That'll keep the small stuff off; anything up to a pinhead – say about the size of Keller's intellect.'

'And the bigger stuff?'

'Come on, kid, you did your theory. See anything bigger'n a golf ball, you can shout "Fore!" and kiss your ass goodbye.'

'Great. He's telling jokes already.'

'What's the matter kid, don't ya have a sense of humour?' You rake the stick to avoid the first of the big rocks, something about as big as one of Habib's 'roo burgers. The rock tumbles backwards and scrapes the trailers with a nerve-wracking squeal before shooting away into space. 'Jeez, kid, how the hell you ever hope to be a Space Trucker if you don't have a sense of humour?'

The kid finally gets the message and shuts up, just in time for the bear to cut in again – this time on the emergency frequency. '*You better power down, Canyon. Power down and pull over. Now.*'

'Sorry boys, got a priority load of perishable goods here. And an expensive cargo.'

'*It's not a request! We got questions about Keller.*'

'Well, boys and girls, last time I seen him he was being sucked ass first into the big dark. You want to join him I suggest you follow us where the sun don't shine. John Canyon and *Bitchin' Betty*, signing off, and I'll see you in hell.'

You tuck *Betty* into the rings proper, goose the afterburners and run like a bastard.

– 5 –

Your name is Arty Renshaw, you're a Peace Officer Grade Three – assigned to mobile duty – and you love a good high-speed chase.

Right at this moment you're approaching the ring system like a bat out of hell, jets flaming, head spinning with the chase, the potential of the arrest, the possible promotion it could bring.

You've got such a buzz on that even if you knew you had less than five minutes to live it wouldn't come close to spoiling the fun.

You don't know, of course.

So you kick in the burners and throttle down the jets and scoot sideways into the murderous field of scrap.

Canyon's rig is dead ahead now, winding between the jagged lumps of almost-planet or ex-moon, edging sideways to move with the orbital drift. You can see what he's doing. Trying to minimise relative delta-vee if he sustains a hit. There's always the odd chunk though. Your own defence system deals with one even as you think about it, leaving you watching floating green blobs for a second before picking up the chase.

By now the chatter or radio traffic is mercifully brief. Cruisers Three, Four and Five are proceeding more cautiously into the ring. They're all older than you. They're all going to live longer too. Even Cruiser Three, his port stabiliser and left arm clipped away by a whirling dervish of ice.

Cruiser Three drops out of the chase with a muttered curse.

You mouth the unofficial motto of the TT: *Kill the baddies, get the girl*.

That's you.

The radio crackles. '*Central to all units. Abandon pursuit. Repeat: do not pursue.*'

You thump the radio. 'I can get them, dammit. They're heading for the Division. If they get out of the system we've lost them for –'

'*Cruiser Two stand down! These orders come from the top: abandon pursuit. Let them go!*'

You shake your head. No way. You heat up the guns. One shot, half power: a disabling blast. You're too close to give up now.

Kill the baddies –

You edge closer.

Kill the baddies, get the girl –

Canyon's tail-glare backlights a curtain of drifting ice. You shoot a way clear through the debris.

One blast slips through the debris and scrapes paint from the rearmost cargo trailer. There's your warning shot, right there.

The rig judders.

You ease up close, one hand on the joystick, the other on the guns.

– the baddies get the –

'Canyon, this is TT Cruiser Two ordering you to power down and pull over. This is not a request. Do you copy?'

Your answer comes in a spurt of hard light from the rear top deck of the trailer. A hatch where no hatch had been only a moment before, an eruption of light and suddenly the Cruiser is coming apart around you.

You die fast; not so fast you don't notice what happens to you.

You get cold, but you don't feel that. Instead you feel a momentary prickling of heat all over. It's not heat, though, it's the blood bursting out of your skin.

You're still telling Canyon to power down and pull over when a froth of air and blood from your lungs steals your voice, and your life with it.

– 6 –

You park *Betty* plumb centre of the Cassini Division and take stock.

The kid says, 'Looks like we lost 'em.'

'They stopped chasing us, you mean.'

Cindy frowns. 'You think someone warned them off?'

You join Cindy in a frown. 'Dunno.'

The kid is still on a buzz from the ride. 'Jeez, man, that was some of the best driving I've ever seen.'

You've never been too clever at accepting compliments. You cut him a thin smile and change the subject.

'Everyone OK?'

'Yeah.'

'Sure'.

Betty spoils the one hundred per cent track-record by pointing out a small problem. You tell the others about it. 'Fuel reserve's down to sixty-eight per cent. One of those rockets must've cracked a line.'

'Can we patch it?'

'No need. Automatics cut in soon as the breach occurred or we'd be dead in space already.'

Your face tells them the rest of the story.

'There is, however, a problem.'

The kid says, 'At max velocity we're still gonna be sixty hours the wrong side of delivery time.'

You sigh. 'Kid, you've been reading the screens again, haven't ya? I told ya: you're passenger, not partner. You do as you're told. Don't try to think on your own. I got enough hassles already.'

'It's true though, ain't it? These old Pachyderms never made much past point oh-two cee. We'll renege on the contract and forfeit our payment.'

You sigh. 'If we stay in the shipping lanes.'

You see by his face that he doesn't get it. You explain it to him, real simple like. 'Yes, these old Pachyderms are slow. Yes, we'll be late. Yes, we'll forfeit our payment.' You pause and then hit him with the solution. 'That's why we're gonna cut a course through the Scum Cluster.'

The look on his face is a mixture of outrage, amazement and terror. It's almost funny.

114

'You can shut your mouth, kid, *Betty* already has a perfectly good insect-killer.' You jerk a thumb at uncle Denny's Venus Flytrap in a little pot velcroed to the inner hull back of the kitchen.

The kid gawps stupidly.

'Catchin' flies – you know?'

His teeth snap together with an audible click.

Cindy demonstrates her smarts by keeping mum. Then again she doesn't have to say anything. You each know what the other is thinking. You all know what happened to Kev the Thief. You all wondered why in hell he made such a dumb choice as to run the Scum Cluster in the first place.

Now you're starting to get the idea of why.

Not that it'll do you any good.

You avoid the incipient argument by the simple expedient of pulling yourself wearily into your bunk and going to sleep.

Bare-Ass

1

You wake up as you always do – in a seriously bad temper. There's a reason for this, and while rigs are built by accountants instead of engineers it's never going to change.

See, it's like this:

The Three Esses: shit, shower and shave. The God-given right of any Terran citizen, you might think. On a planet, in positive-g, you'd be right.

In space, it's not that easy.

Showering is a non-starter because of the necessity for conservation of water. Shaving ditto. This makes the average rig a breeding-ground for the kind of smells which a skunk would feel at home in – and which over the years have doubled the demand for nasal nerve-ending cauterisation. (The cost of surgery being about half the cost of installing a top-flight aircon system in your average rig.)

The third S is more problematical. Wisely you just scoot through the necessary procedures as quickly as possible – trying not to dwell on the possible consequences of a malfunction in the soil reclamation plant – and then get on with breakfast.

This consists of nuking squeeze-tubes of various flavoured pastes in Aunt Hettie's microwave and then squishing one after another into your mouth: again, as quickly as possible. In space, nutrition is all-important and flavour seems to come a very poor last.

This morning, breakfast comprises mixed-cereal-paste washed down by orange-juice-paste followed by bacon-lettuce-and-tomato-bun-paste and a side order of jam-on-toasted-waffles-paste.

As usual, all you can taste is the inside of the tubes.

Also as usual, you've managed to precisely miss that fine line between graveyard-at-midnight cold and engines-on-meltdown heat which most microwaves – particularly Aunt Hettie's – seem to have as their only two settings. The result of which is that you scald your tongue on the orange-juice-paste and almost break your only remaining real tooth on a squeeze-tube-shaped bacon-and-lettuce-and-tomato popsicle.

You nuke a cappuccino-tube to take away the taste of microwaved polythene. In space coffee is your die-hard companion; the one flavour even purification, desiccation and storage for half a year within plastic squeeze-tubes cannot compromise.

You swallow with an effort and the paste – sorry, *food* – begins its long journey downwards.

Its long, queasy journey downwards.

Ignoring a message from your lower intestine indicating that a repeat performance of the most socially compromising of the Three Esses may soon be required, you call Cindy and the kid to breakfast.

While they're rubbing sleepy dust from their eyes and – judging by the kid's protesting groans – waking from at least one seriously wet dream, you perform the morning rounds.

You dust your lucky Gibson twelve-string. You re-arrange the darts in your lucky dartboard to Monday's position. You feed Uncle Denny's Venus Flytrap with a couple of choice morsels found squashed into the soles of your boots after the chase through SkyTown's sewers.

The coffee is kicking in by now. Your head's losing that last sleepy fuzziness and your limbs are beginning to shake with the caffeine rush.

You let the coffee run your system for a while then head back to the 'pit. Daily rituals complete, you can now get down to the serious business of worrying about your impending transit of the Scum Cluster.

Cindy and the kid are gulping silently on the squeeze-tubes of food. It tends to kill conversation like that.

After a moment Cindy makes a face, spits out a glob of food, bats it towards the waste recycler chute. 'John, how long have you had this crap?'

'Forever and a day,' the kid mutters through clenched teeth. 'Least that's what it tastes like.'

'We on time?' Cindy adds, concern for her mother edging her voice.

'We will be if we make it through the Cluster.'

Something bangs hard against the windscreen. You jump nervously. You look through the windscreen. They follow your gaze. The thing that went bag was a spacesuit. It bounces from the rig and tumbles away into space.

'Did you see that?'

'It was ripped to pieces.'

'Was there anyone in it?'

'If there was they were hog-fodder.'

'Jeez Louise.'

A long silence.

As if the suit is a signal, more debris begins to bump the rig. Gloves, a smashed helmet, a burnt spaceboot, an oxygen cylinder dribbling icy crystals, a computer mainframe with an orbiting asteroid belt of disks, a desiccated pot-plant, a cracked urinal. Bits and pieces of a black flapping substance that might once have been human flesh, now alternately burnt and frozen by direct sunlight and exposure to the big dark.

The hull rattles with impacts. The radar blips like an alarm clock.

The kid looks sick. Cindy is expressionless.

'It must have been a big ship.'

'What do you think happened to it?'

'Jackers, obviously.'

'Jeez Louise.'

The noise against the hull increases suddenly; *Betty* screeches an insistent warning.

The kid is staring out of the windscreen. 'I don't see no density ten asteroid field. Your rig's on the blink –'

'Shut up kid.' You stare out of the windscreen too. Nothing. Just jackers trash and the stars glimmering distantly in the –

Wait a minute.

Stars don't glimmer. Not in space. Not unless their light is being reflected off something, that is. Something invisible to the naked eye. Something like –

'Christ on his great steel wheels, it's black rock! Collar up!'

Without waiting to check on the others, you grab the stick and punch in the afterburners. *Betty* is squealing distances and vectors in a panicky voice. The kid is yelling advice you don't need. The angry roar of Old Man Universe is loud in your head.

Only Cindy is quiet. You follow her example.

Ignoring the noisy chaos you yank *Betty* around and head upwards, out of the plane of the ecliptic.

If you just got to the stick in time –

If the belt is flat enough –

If it's your lucky day –

You didn't. It's not. It's definitely not.

A chunk of black rock as big as a freight car lurches out of the big dark. *Betty* screeches a collision alarm. You bruise your hand on the stick. The thrusters are hot. Maybe you'll make it.

You almost do. Then more rock hurls itself out of nowhere and the resultant collision sends a mountain of jagged boulders shooting your way.

With the kind of luck that makes insurance executives reach gibbering for their ulcer medication, almost all of it hits you.

– 2 –

You wake up, sit up, bounce off the ceiling. Cindy and the kid are already awake. The kid is mopping up trash – about a ton of trash knocked loose by the multiple collision – and shoving it all willy-nilly back into the space where the refrigerator would be if you bought extras.

'Go easy with the goddamn cribbage board, willya kid? Those matches are genuine antiques.'

The kid grunts something unintelligible in reply. It's probably nothing nice.

Betty is quiet. Too quiet.

When you ask her what's up, she tells you in a voice that's almost apologetic. 'Main and secondary engines are down due to pressure constriction of components in directional control systems located aft of bulkhead three in the secondary thruster chamber . . .' She drones on, enhancing the lecture with fancy graphics.

You get the gist without much bother.

'Some dumb rock knocked a damn great hole in you, *Betty*, am I right?'

Betty agrees, then adds more bad news. 'Internal coolant systems have also sustained damage and are currently non-operational.'

'So we're toast?'

'Shut up, kid.'

'– and power to the urinal recycler unit has been diverted to maintain emergency lighting and cabin pressure.'

'Fuckin' A!'

'I said shut up, kid.'

Cindy catches your eye. 'It's already getting hot in here. No chance of a fix?'

You ask *Betty*, then relay the answer. 'Sure there is. After a five-hour cooldown.'

The kid is already starting to sweat. 'We'll roast in here by then.'

'What about an SOS?'

'What about it?'

'Well, we could broadcast one, right?'

'And have it ignored. It's the Transport Commission's policy to disregard distress signals from the Scum Cluster.'

'That's crap! Why?'

Cindy tells him. 'Because it could be an ambush. Right, John?'

You nod.

The kid sniffs, wipes a hand across his forehead. 'Yeah, well, maybe another driver might render aid – you know, like a human being?'

You laugh. 'A good Samaritan? In the Scum Cluster? Let me tell you something kid. The only traffic out there is Company traffic and the nearest shipping lane is a half a dozen AUs off at best, and anyway, the least human thing I can think of right now is a Company driver. And they don't answer distress calls either, because time is money and the last thing they need in their rig is more mouths to gulp their air and make them late and jeopardise their pay packet.'

The kid frowns. 'You have a bleak view of humanity, John.'

'I have a bleak view of everything, son.'

Cindy wipes her face on her sleeve. She doesn't need to state the obvious. *Betty*'ll be joining in with a rash of systems failure warnings anytime now.

You suppose it's just dumb luck that none of the rocks breached the hull.

The kid suddenly grins. 'What about the escape pod?'

'Only holds two.'

'We could draw straws.'

'And I could toss you out the airlock for making a dumb-ass suggestion like that.'

'So that's it then? We're gonna die?'

You shrug. 'Nope. We got a little juice in the parking rockets. If we cut the load loose we might be able to put ourselves in the shadow on one of those asteroids.'

'Means we lose our commission.'

'I'm starting to think that's a way of life. You in or out?'

'Like I have a choice?'

'Always choices, kid. Long as you live and breathe.'

'You some kinda optimist, John?'

'Watch the insults, kid, or you can walk the rest of the way to Earth.'

'Sure.'

Cindy cuts off your angry reply with a look. 'John, don't. It's the heat talking, right?'

You nod, unbunch fists you didn't realise were clenched. 'Sure, Cindy. Whatever you say.'

The kid sees sense as well. 'Using a rock for shadow, that's a good idea. It might buy us enough time to fix the engines.' He pulls himself towards the airlock. 'I'll help you jettison the load.'

You get there first. 'It's a one-man job.'

There's more bad news waiting for you outside the rig.

The leading cargo trailer has extruded a set of metallic clamps. They completely cover *Betty*'s own cargo clamps. There's no sign of wiring conduit, nothing you can cut. The only apparent answer is to take the metal-cutter from the tool-kit and cut loose both sets of clamps together. You get the cutter out, scowling. Another cost. Damn this load.

You fire up the cutter and hold it against the clamps. It skids straight off, nearly taking a chunk out of your suit as it does. You swear. At once the kid's on the radio. '*Anything I can do to help, John?*'

'Yeah. You can stop whining in my ear while I'm trying to work!'

You change the contacts on the cutter, up the juice and try again.

Nothing.

Well, not quite nothing.

Either side of the trailer two previously invisible hatches slide open. They're like two dark eyes staring at you.

You don't like this, not one little bit.

The eyes blink. No, not blink – something's

emerging. Two somethings. Two somethings that look enough like self-targeting weapons so that your suit soil-reclaimers go into immediate overdrive.

The weapons lock on to you.

Your body acts without your mind slowing it down with useless instructions to *get out, get out now before the damn thing blasts you to the other side of hell* and you're moving.

Not away.

Towards the trailer.

You sit on the cargo clamp.

The guns move, lightning flashes, absolutely silent in the big dark. The blasts would have vaporised you if you'd tried to get away. Instead they take out a reasonable-sized chunk of *Betty*'s hull and expose deeply buried circuitry. You feel the shock transmitted to you through the skin of the ship and it sounds like distant thunder.

You're pissed off now.

And the kid's on the blower again. '*What the hell was that John? We got more black rock out there?*'

'That, kid, was what happened to the bears chasing us.'

'*You what?*'

'Never mind, kid. Stay inside. I'll get back to you.'

You don't move. You stay absolutely still. The

126

guns cannot shoot you because if they do they'll be shooting at the cargo trailer as well.

You try a slight movement – one hand grasping and a slight pull sideways, out of the line of fire. The guns track you.

You stop. So do they.

You move. So do they. This time they fire. The arm of your suit sizzles. Inside the air heats up fast, and your arm with it.

You withdraw and the guns stop firing. You examine the sleeve. The suit's outer armour is gone, puffed to vapour. You're lucky the sleeve can still hold air. You look at the guns thoughtfully. Lucky? No way. Near miss? Again – no way. These things are smart – smarter and faster than Aunt Hettie's accountant. They didn't miss; the part of you they hit was the only part in a legitimate killzone.

You sit still, wrap your legs around the clamp. You have about fifty minutes of air in the backpack. Enough time to think a way out of this mess? Maybe.

Perhaps if you stay still long enough the guns will think you've gone away and do the same.

Good plan.

Suddenly there is a tearing sound and a hiss. Your ears pop. The suit sleeve has given way. You're losing pressure.

You reach for the patchkit in your backpack.

127

The guns track your arm's movement. You whip it back to your side, fast. The guns stop.

You wait.

Your arm feels like red hot needles are being shoved in it by some insane acupuncturist.

You wait.

Your breath is coming harder as the air thins. Your ears are beginning to hurt.

You call the kid for help.

There's no answer.

You wait.

So do the guns.

Ah well. It was a good plan as far as it went.

– 3 –

Afterwards both of you would blame the heat. But would that really be fair? Fair to John, or to yourselves?

It started innocently enough – a conversation, nothing special, this, that, who, how. 'You were born on Earth, weren't you?'

You watch her nod. The elegance. The curve of her neck. The arch of her brow. 'Yeah. New York, through and through, that's me.' She looks concerned. 'You can't tell, right? I've been working on losing the accent.'

You crack a grin. 'Slow job then.' You clock her look, rush to add, 'Oh but it's OK, I mean, it's a cool accent.'

'Yeah?'

'Yeah.'

She thinks about that for a while. Both of you are collared in to the co-pilot seats. Now she pushes up the collar, stretches.

'Jeez, it's hot.'

You ask *Betty* for a heat projection curve. She obliges. It's not good news.

Another glance at Cindy. Can you trust her with the dream? The one you've had since childhood? 'What's it like on Earth? I always dreamed about seeing the place. You know. Trees, birds . . . those . . . uh . . . those things that live in rivers.'

She smiles. 'You mean fish, right?' The smile turns wistful. 'Yeah. My mother took me to the oceanarium in New York. I used to call it the Wet Museum. You know, as opposed to normal museum, with dry stuff in it.' She giggles. 'They have all sorts of fish there. They can protect them. The rivers . . . you know, they're too dirty. Or something.'

'That's a shame.'

'I don't know. What self-respecting fish would want to live in a dirty old river anyway, right?' She shrugs. 'What about you?'

'Do I want to live in a dirty old river?' She rewards you with another laugh. 'I was born on Titan. Parents worked in the Genesis Lab. Heads full of amino acid chains and tame lightning and never a moment for baby Michael.' You chew on your lip for a moment, memories crowding in. 'They were so obsessed with the idea of creating life on Titan that they never noticed the life they had already created there.'

'Oh Mike, that's sad.'

'Well, it's hard to miss what you never had, right? I had enough to keep me occupied – for a while. Then Dad died and Mum was promoted and that was that – I hauled ass outta there and . . . well, here I am.'

'A Space Trucker.'

She says the word proudly. Touches the sleeve of your pink jacket tenderly. Or distractedly. Something. There's a weird feeling in the pit of your stomach. If you weren't in zero-g you'd say you'd just gone weightless.

'My day died too . . . not long after I turned six . . .' She pulls herself together with an effort. 'I can see why you'd think that New York was an amazing place. It was, I guess.'

'But you left though.'

The sad look was back. 'I didn't want to. My Dad always used to say the rest of the Earth – the rest of the system – was for hicks. No offence,' she adds quickly, perhaps guiltily, following it up with a smile. 'In any case, I don't believe that, do you?'

'Nah.'

'After Dad died, Mum got sick. I think she got it from a river where she took me one day. I'm not sure, and the doctors only ever said one thing I could understand.' She hesitates, seeming to look inwards, and back through the years. 'Mum knew her health . . . well, it would only get worse. So when I was ten she used the last of our money to get me into an engineering programme off-world.' Cindy adjusts her blouse. The movement reminds you of how damp your own clothes are, how they are clinging to you. 'But I flunked the course. They say girls are better at it because of the way their heads are wired, or something, I dunno. . . . All that's crap though, right? You are what you are, I say. And I was never meant to be a spanner-jockey, I guess. So anyways, I got trained up as a waitress and ended up at SkyTown.'

'You like that?'

'Nah, it sucks. If I had the money I'd go back to school. Get qualified.'

'What in?'

'I don't know. Anything. Art, maybe. Hairdressing. Something like that. My Dad always said, "Be a hairdresser or an undertaker. Either one, you're never short of work." And anything's better than waiting tables.' An idea strikes her. 'Hey – maybe I could be a Space Trucker.'

'With John?'

She looks at you strangely. 'Mike Pucci, for a man who's never seen a river you're mighty good at fishing.'

'Yeah?'

She sniffs, runs the back of her arm across her brow. 'Yeah. As in, finding out what the deal is between me and John.'

'So what is the deal between you and John?'

'We had a history, alright? He's into me. And he's a nice man. A little old but a nice man. I could do worse.'

'You could do better, too.'

'Like you, you mean?'

'Well . . . yeah, since you mention it.'

'Yeah, well, don't think I don't see the merit in what you're saying.' She hesitates. Adds, 'Thing is, I promised him I'd marry him if he got me to Earth. And I keep my promises.'

'Yeah?'

'Yeah.'

'You always take life so seriously?'

'Always.' Her answer is firm. So is her voice.

'That's OK then . . .'

'Yeah?'

'Sure.' You add, deadpan, 'As long as you want Canyon for his body I don't have to worry that you're gonna milk him for his trucking experience and get qualified and beat me to the next load, right?'

She cannot decide what to make of that one.

'Competition. Can't stand it, y'see. I'm ambitious.'

'Yeah?'

'Oh yeah.'

There's a moment of silence.

'You're joking right?'

'Am I?' You wait just the right amount of time, then add, 'Anyway, Space Truckers get lousy tips.'

There's relief in her laughter. 'I noticed.'

The laugh is infectious. A moment later you're both bawling your eyes out with hysterical tears.

'Jeez, I gotta ditch this shirt.' You pull it off. Stop half way, aware of her look. 'That's OK with you, right?'

'Oh sure.'

'Cool.' The shirt comes off.

So does hers.

You blink. For about a minute there are no thoughts in your head at all. Nothing. No awareness of heat. No smells, no little noises. Nothing. Your head is a big empty space full of her, the sight of her.

She looks at you. 'Do *you* mind?'

'Uh no . . . 'course not . . . I . . . uh . . . sorry. I was staring, wasn't I?'

'Well, yeah. You were, kinda.' She shrugs.

133

'What the hell. It's OK, I guess. It's not like we ain't friends or nothing.'

You swallow. 'Are we friends?'

She grins. 'John's right. You do say dumb things sometimes.'

To cover your embarrassment you yank off your boots and trousers. It's not until her grin widens that you realise what you have done. But by then it's too late. She has undressed as well.

That's when it all gets confusing. You've taken your clothes off so you should feel cooler but you don't. You're hotter. And even more constricted than ever. And you can't draw your breath.

After a moment you realise it's because she's holding you.

And kissing you.

Eventually she lets you go. 'My lips are tingling. Either the air in here is running out and I'm cyanotic, or –'

That's all you let her say for a while.

Once again your head is empty. All thought of cash, cargo, delivery dates, Scum Cluster, black rock, guilt, morality, living, dying; all gone.

Instead there's her. Just her.

For a while, it's enough.

– 4 –

The solution to your problem presents itself, like

the solutions to a great many of life's problems, almost accidentally.

A Castlemaine XXXX six-pack, jacker trash, drifting through the big dark, and into the path of the weapons trained on you.

The guns track the beer.

They do not fire.

The beer drifts towards you.

The guns wait.

The beer drifts right past you, scrapes across the cargo clamps, bounces off *Betty*'s hull.

Still the guns don't fire.

You can't believe they're smart enough to determine motivation. Perhaps they can distinguish between a six-pack of beer and a man in a spacesuit. There's a hundred ways they could do that.

That would make them real smart guns though.

Maybe it's not that they're programmed to destroy anything which threatens the cargo. Maybe it's that they're programmed to destroy anything trying simply to *unhitch* the cargo.

You open your gloved hand and the six-pack settles neatly into it. The other arm is numb from the elbow down. Pins and needles are working their way up towards your shoulder. Autoclamps have sealed the suit – but you're gonna lose the arm if you don't get into positive pressure soon.

As soon as you touch the beer, the guns twist, eagerly seeking a target lock. Logical. They now read the can as part of you. And your motivation was clear from the moment you stepped out of *Betty*'s airlock.

Motivation. That's the key.

You've got a plan.

Clutching the six-pack to your chest, you offer a short prayer to the gods of the big dark that, just this once, your mind, incapable as it is normally of finishing more than one crossword in a decade, hasn't muffed the easy clue this time.

You push yourself off the trailer, out into the big dark.

The guns track you . . .

. . . track you . . .

. . . then fold neatly away into their holes, harmless as a child's new toy.

'Jeez!' You feel like puking in your suit. 'Zesty you old bugger, if you wasn't dead already I'd kill you myself.'

Two minutes later your suit sleeve is patched and feeling is returning to your arm – and don't you wish it weren't.

That's the good news.

The bad news comes ten minutes later when you cycle back through the lock and dump your suit.

And see Cindy and the kid wearing less than a broken clothes-horse.

Somehow you get the feeling that if you'd got back even a minute earlier you might have seen them wearing little except each other.

You try to contain your surprise. Your anger.

You don't try too hard.

'Hot in here, right?'

the kid has the grace to look sheepish. 'Yeah.'

Cindy says nothing.

'So we take our clothes off.' You check out your arm. It's covered in decompression blisters from elbow to wrist. It hurts like a bastard – but it doesn't look like it's going to fall off anytime soon. You show them the arm. 'Stay comfortable, right?'

'Yeah.'

Cindy reaches for your arm but you pull it back. 'Would that have been your idea?'

The kid butts in with, 'It was my idea. So what?'

You shrug. Then turn, fix the kid with a glare that has preceded many different types of trouble in the past. 'It's just that it's a pretty cheesy way of getting a look at my girlfriend's particulars.'

'Now hold on John, that ain't what's going on here.'

'No? "We're gonna die and this is my last

137

chance for a piece of ass, what about it?" I gotta
hand it to ya kid, you're the king of the smooth
talkers. "It's getting hot in here, your husband's
outside getting his hand shot off –"'

'We ain't married, buddy!'

'– so you can have a few extra minutes of life –'

'You want to know what I think of a guy who
forces a girl to marry him in exchange for giving
her a ride –'

'– and whaddaya do with them? Ya do this!'
The anger turns into self-pity – and that turns
straight back into anger again – doubled this
time. Cindy is babbling something. You can't
hear it. You can't hear anything. You swing over
to the kid. He holds his ground. He thinks you're
an old bear and he thinks he's gonna pull your
teeth but he's got another think coming and
that's no word of a lie –

'*For crying out loud will you both shut up!*'
Cindy's voice is a roar. Surprised, you do exactly
as she says. So does the kid. 'Real smart men
aren't ya? Fighting over a girl who'll be two
scoops of ash in two hours? Huh? We're all
gonna be dead soon – maybe we could try for a
degree of dignity here.'

It isn't a question and no-one treats it as if it is.

You sit down.

'It is pretty damned hot in here.'

The kid stares at you. If he's hoping for an

apology that's the best you can be bothered with.

He unclenches his fists. 'Did you get the load unhooked?'

You hold up your arm. 'Whaddaya think this is, kid, sunburn? There's some kinda auto-defence deal hooked into the trailer. Smartguns.'

The kid sits down too. 'Whatever's in those trailers, it ain't no sex dolls. A plastic date doesn't need that kinda protection.'

Cindy says, 'Why don't we divert the coolant from the refrigerator through the inside plumbing?'

The kid looks hopeful. 'Who said you couldn't be an engineer?'

You say wearily, 'I do. See that space over there beside the microwave. That space you shoved all that loose trash into earlier?'

'Yeah.'

'That space with plumbing for a refrigerator?'

The kid cottons on fast. 'You don't have a refrigerator?'

'What the hell you suppose I use the double glazing for? I told ya kid. The fridge was an option – I don't buy options.'

'Great.'

'But I did bring this.'

You produce the Castlemaine XXXX six-pack.

'It won't save your life, kid, but it will make you feel better.'

'Great.'

The beer is still partly frozen. You crack three cans and suck beer popsicles.

'You know,' you mutter sluggishly some time later. 'I would have liked to have made it.' You burp. 'Probably would've made a lousy husband though.'

You're not so drunk you miss the guilty looks they exchange.

You don't miss the shadow that falls over the windscreen either.

After a moment they notice it too.

Outside the window is a twelve-mile-long nightmare decked out in space-black armour, smothered with lights, cranes, gunports. Lots of gunports. An Oligarch-Lines logo has been clumsily replaced by a quarter-mile long skull-and-crossbones.

'Jeez Louise – it's the goddamn *Regalia*!'

'The jackers!'

You crunch a mouthful of beer popsicle. 'Kid, you've no idea how lucky you are you're not wearing those pink Company pyjamas.'

– 5 –

You don't need to see outside to know what's going on. The *Regalia* could swallow twenty rigs

140

like *Betty* and their cargoes and still only half-fill its cargo deck.

That's what it does, in ponderous slow motion, silent, inevitable, unstoppable.

You don't hear the stadium-sized hatch slam shut, but you feel the crash as the cargo deck spins up to provide artificial gravity.

It takes an hour to pressurise the cargo deck and fifteen minutes to cut the power lines to *Betty*'s airlock. All that time you can hear them working. Distant shouts and curses, gonging sounds of metal on metal, the hiss and crackle of cutters.

And laughter.

If spiders could laugh it would sound like this.

The kid snaps pretty soon.

Rummaging in the junk cupboard where the refrigerator should have been, he comes up with your Uncle Hector's gun. The one from the war. The one that supposedly saved the life of the Seceding Venusian Colony President's life.

Cindy watches this in silence.

The kid waves the gun about. She watches this too.

'John. You got any more like this?'

'Ain't even sure this one works. It was Uncle Hector's. Last time it was fired was probably a decade ago.'

Cindy chips in with pertinent information. 'They'll be through the hatch in two minutes.'

You're still riding the kid. 'You gonna make one of those famous last stands?'

'Setting aside what these scum might have in mind for us, what do you think they're going to do to –' A nod towards Cindy. The look on her face suggests that under those conditions it might be better to worry about what she would do to them.

She glares at the kid. 'What do you have in mind, Mike? Save the last two shots for us and hope the gun doesn't blow up in your face?'

That stumps him.

They choose that moment to bust through the airlock. The first jacker through the hatch is faced with the three of you, one clutching a big gun, one clutching a Gibson twelve-string like a billy club and the other holding a beer popsicle.

The jacker you are faced with is seven feet tall, hair down to his ass and a face much as one would suppose his ass to look like, judging by the rest of him. He looks at Cindy twice. Once with his eyes, once with his gun. Filthy clothes, filthy mind, filthy tongue.

'Put down the guitar, girlie. You I could play with but the twelve-string is irreplaceable.'

Prudently, Cindy obeys.

More jackers join the party. One is as wide as Ass-face is tall, painfully pretty in the way fat people can be, weight doubled by the rings piercing every visible piece of bare flesh; the other is almost normal-looking, except for his nose. It's been replaced by a triangular piece of gold mirrorglass.

Like Ass-face, both Rings and Nose have *enormous* guns.

They point them at the kid.

He shrugs, lifts his own gun, starts firing.

The magazine sputters and fizzes.

That's all.

Laughing, Ass-face says, 'Congratulations, you are now prisoners of the *Regalia*. If you resist, I'll kill you. If you try to escape, I'll kill you. If you argue, I'll kill you.' He stares at Cindy again. 'If you try to get dressed, I'll kill you.'

Then he looks at the kid and smiles. 'That goes for you too, loverboy.'

The other jackers laugh.

'You can keep the gun if you like. A reminder of the last day of your life.'

You hold out the beer popsicle. 'Do I get killed if I offer you gentlemen a beer?'

Ass-face looks at you. 'Well, whaddaya know, the famous John Canyon. I heard you were dead. Fuck with me and you will be. Now what was that you said about a beer?'

Scum

Emerging from the rig is like walking out of a closet into a junkyard the size of a football stadium.

The cargo deck is a cylinder built around the *Regalia*'s central core. It's nearly a mile in diameter. There are clouds in here. About thirty degrees of arc away it's raining on three junked rigs. More rigs, gutted hulks in various states of dismemberment, together with the remains of their cargoes, are scattered in hillocks and escarpments across the rising horizon. Cranes and loaders drift lazily from one work site to another. All of them seem to have ghetto-blasters fitted as standard. Jackers operating cutters and drills are busy slicing into the hull plates of the as-yet-intact cargo trailers. Sparks skitter across the deck as saws bite. Metal tears, screeching. More crates spill out to join the mess of empty containers piled up across the entire cargo deck, in some places to a height of several storeys.

And the place stinks. Grease, sweat, steam, the

mould scabbing oil-slicked puddles, burning acetylene, hot steel, electricity.

And something else. A smell you don't want to think too much about.

Blood.

As you watch, a cargo-lifter blows a side-thruster. The crane tumbles, crates hit the deck and split. A mess of animals – they look like cows – slide out and into the nearby jackers. Laughter at the fate of the crane driver turns to yells of annoyance as some of the jackers are trampled by the terrified cows. The rest pull themselves together, fire up their cutters and run, whooping madly, in search of steak dinners.

The jackers themselves are a mixed bunch. Their clothes range from Neanderthal to fashionably post-modern. Ditto their personal decoration. You suppose it's all down to who they last jacked. There are men and women – some are indistinguishable – but all have one thing in common.

Whatever they're doing, they're doing it to excess.

Ass-face gives the three of you a moment to take this in and then prods you at gunpoint away from the rig. Once clear it's easy to see how much the worse for wear *Betty* is. She was never designed for gravity. Now the cargo deck's up to spin she's looking very poorly indeed. She's canted over to one side, cargo trailers twisted in a metal braid as long as a football field. Jackers are already at work on the trailers, cutting torches blazing. You try not to imagine the torque the trailers are exerting on the cargo clamps. One thing's for sure: if the clamps do go at least you'll be able to leave the damn cargo here when you do leave – if you leave.

That's something that Ass-face, Rings and Nose don't seem particularly keen on at the moment.

As if deciding his welcoming speech was enough homeliness and friendliness for the time being, Ass-face pushes you through the churning mess of noise and activity towards a gallows pole with, coincidentally, three sets of wrist-irons hanging from it.

Actually there are four sets but one is currently occupied by what looks like a set of dirty laundry. Only as you approach do you see it's a corpse dressed in Interpork pink. The driver's face has been ripped and twisted into a bloody parody of a hog's muzzle, the eyes punched in, the nose hammered flat, the ears peeled from the skull to hang in pointed flaps.

You try not to puke. It would be hard at the best of times and the smell makes it harder. You manage the trick with some difficulty. The kid is not so successful. He sets off Cindy – and between them you lose it as well.

Breakfast is about as pleasant coming up as it was going down.

When you've finished, all three of you are fastened into the irons and hoisted about an inch clear of the ground.

It isn't a very pleasant experience. Your arms are in immediate pain. Muscles you've forgotten about over the years remind you of their presence by telling you how much more pain you are going to be in within a very short time.

If you stand on tiptoes you can alleviate the pain slightly.

Then your legs start to hurt.

Rings and Nose wander off in the direction of your rig. Ass-face dispenses orders to nearby jackers with distressing clarity.

'Oy you! Go with Rings and Nose; help them gut the new salvage. I want the rig gutted; these guys ain't gonna need it no more. And you. Yes, you, idiot, quit playing with yourself. Run along like a good fellow and tell the Captain we've got friends for dinner.'

A jacker laughs at what is clearly an in-joke and runs off, clattering through the piles of junk.

'And you, Wankbreath! Get the cutlery. Don't forget the knives. And those dentist's wotsits. And the saw. And that cattleprod thingy. And make sure it's charged or you'll be wearing it as an anal decoration.'

Another minion cackles inanely as he runs off into the echoing bowels of the ship.

It wouldn't be funny, even if your wrists weren't chained and bleeding, and every muscle in your back and legs wasn't tying itself into agonising knots.

Ass-face turns towards a nearby jacker who is using an oxy-cutter to unstitch sections of hullplate from one of the wrecks. Ass-face grabs the cutter, uses it to light a cigarette. When the jacker protests, Ass-face gives him a look you could have told him means trouble. Big trouble.

The jacker is too dumb to notice. 'Hey, asshole, you want my fucking torch? Hey, why not have my fucking balls too? What about my fucking sister, you want her as well? I tell you, you fuck with me and I'll fuck you right up. You got that? Now I got a job to do here, so give me back my fucking torch.'

Ass-face listens calmly to the stream of invective, then shrugs. 'Your balls you can keep, they're really too small to interest me. Your sister, well she's had everyone on the ship so I'd probably catch something from her, and anyway, being as how she's related to you I expect she's roughly half as smart as my kid's Speak-and-Spell, which I'm sure you'll agree makes her a poor choice of life companion.'

By now the jacker is on his feet, fuming. He

reaches for something. A knife, or maybe a gun. Before the move is half finished Ass-face is talking again.

'As for your torch. Yes, you are quite correct. I do have it. You want it back? That's fine with me.' Ass-face lets the jacker have his torch back.

Right in the face.

One eye fizzes into slush right away, along with half the nose and most of the left cheek. Fingers from the hands which jerk instinctively to cover the wound patter softly to the deck. There's not much blood; the wounds cauterise fast.

'Hey, Butch!' Ass-face calls above the jackers agonised screams. 'Dinner time, boy.'

A dog ambles out from behind the engine section of a cargo crane and begins to chew on the burnt fingers. The dog is a mongrel, sleek and healthy looking, obviously better fed than most of the crew. That's not surprising when you consider it has probably dined on many of them. Or at least parts of them.

The kid makes a gagging sound.

Cindy says nothing.

The jacker is on the deck by now, writhing in pain. He's close to passing out when Ass-face jerks the torch near his face again. 'Hey guy, you in pain? You hurt yourself? Anything I can do for you?' He stands, shouts across the cargo deck,

'There's a man in pain here. Somebody get this guy some aspirin.'

He laughs; nobody moves.

At least, nobody moves to help.

Ass-face shrugs. 'Sorry, guy, guess we're fresh outta aspirin.'

The jacker has stopped screaming now. Unconscious or dead, there's no way of telling from where you are.

Ass-face sucks on his cigarette, turns his attention back to you. Well, to be strictly accurate his attention is divided between Cindy and the kid. He seems to be trying to make up his mind about something. You try not to think about what that something might be.

What's worrying you most is the distracted way he's holding the oxy-cutter, bouncing it idly from palm to palm whilst belching huge gobbets of cigarette smoke through the flame.

It's through the smoke that he turns his attention from Cindy and the kid to you. 'John Canyon. I respect you, man. You're a legend. Well, bearing in mind you're dead, of course.' He sucks thoughtfully on his cigarette, jams the butt into the eyesocket of the corpse hanging next to you and lights another with the cutter. ''Course, since you are dead, there'd be nobody to complain if I killed you again, would there?'

The question's rhetorical. You're past caring.

'Listen, man, I gotta lotta respect for you guys too. All of you, living out here like this. It's the frontier, and what with everybody hating you and all. But I can see that you're hard-working folks. So if you'd just get round to making your point I could answer your question and then you wouldn't have to fry my nuts with that thing. OK?'

Ass-face grins, cigarette clamped in perfectly even, white teeth. Some part of your mind is asking itself hysterically how he keeps his teeth so well out here. Another part of your mind is telling the first part to shut the fuck up and get on with the business of getting the rest of you out of this. Between the two it's hard enough to hear yourself think, let alone what Ass-face says next.

'I'm sorry, I was busy panicking. What was that you said?'

He blinks. Obviously not used to being ignored. Oh dear.

I said, 'What're you hauling, Canyon?'

Oh thank you, Lord. An easy one. Maybe you'll all get out of this alive after all. 'We don't know.'

Ass-face's smile fades. He turns up the heat on the cutter and takes a step closer.

Shit.

'I'm telling you we don't know. We never cared.'

151

Ass-face burns away one leg of your trousers. 'It's a mistake to give up caring.'

You can't help screeching. 'Fuck that's hot.'

Ass-face smiles again. 'For a dead man you're pretty funny, Canyon.'

At that moment Rings and Nose hurry back. Nose is clutching Uncle Denny's Venus Flytrap. Rings is waving the cargo manifest Zesty gave you.

Ass-face turns to the jackers. To Nose he says, 'Sometimes I think your brain got vaporised along with your nose. The last thing we need is another mouth to feed. Let alone seven.' He turns the torch on Uncle Denny's Venus Flytrap, burning it and a sizeable portion of Nose's hand when he's too stupid to let go. Ass-face turns to Rings and grabs the manifest. 'This, however, is much more interesting.' Ignoring Nose's heartbroken look, he reads the manifest. He turns to you.

'Now then. This here cargo says you're carrying sex dolls.' He sucks on his cigarette. 'Unless you want to join your green friend here –' he flicks ash at the charred remains of Uncle Denny's Venus Flytrap '– in pot-plant heaven, I suggest you tell me what you're really carrying.'

Unable to contain his anticipation of your answer, Rings wobbles from side to side. 'It's got to be something hot. Maybe it's drugs. Hey, Nose, you like drugs or guns best?'

Nose wrings his burnt hand and glares at Ass-face. 'Right at this moment it's a toss-up.'

Ass-face waves the oxy-cutter in their direction and they scuttle off fast into the maze of cargo crates.

Ass-face turns back to you, but is interrupted again, this time by another jacker pushing a waiter's food trolley covered by a dilapidated linen cloth bearing the Oligarch-Lines logo and a hand-stitched *Regalia* insignia. Beneath the cloth the trolley clinks and clatters in a way which, under the circumstances, you find nerve-racking in the extreme.

'Hey, Wankbreath, you get all the cutlery?'

'Yeah. And the electric thing like you wanted. And it's charged.'

'Good.'

'And the Cap'n's on his way.'

'Good. Now fuck off.'

Ass-face turns back to you, holding the manifest as a prelude to further questioning. He obviously takes it for granted that Wankbreath is going to leave. But Wankbreath has other plans. He's staring at Cindy. He's breathing hard. Abruptly he moves towards her.

Your attention is on Ass-face so you nearly miss the first part of it.

Wankbreath unlocks Cindy's left wrist, takes her hand and shoves it down his pants. He's breathing real hard now. 'Shake hands with the unemployed, baby,' he says in a breathless whisper.

You and Ass-face turn as one, just in time to see Cindy smack her forehead into Wankbreath's face. Blood spurts. You can hear his nose shatter with a sound like snapping toothpicks. His face frozen into a mask of surprise, Wankbreath falls over, poleaxed.

Cindy examines her hand as if something might be growing on it. 'I hope that fucker wasn't infectious.'

Wankbreath tries to rise, can't make it, falls back to the deck. He offers up a surprised little sigh and stops breathing.

After a moment, Rings wobbles out of the sidelines and prods Wankbreath. He doesn't move. Ass-face's mongrel ambles curiously over and makes his own inspection. Still he doesn't move.

When he speaks, Rings' voice quivers as much as his belly. 'He's dead. Wanky's dead. She done killed him.'

Indeed, you can see bone splinters emerging from Wankbreath's face. Splinters you imagine being driven back into his frontal lobes with all the force of a woman's anger behind them.

Ass-face sighs, sucks on his cigarette. He turns to stare at you. 'Ah shit. If I'd known we'd be one mouth less to feed I wouldn't have fried you pot plant.'

You stare at Cindy. No time to wonder how she's taking this. In fact you get a real strong feeling there's not much time left for anything else at all.

Ass-face turns back to you and he's still holding the oxy-cutter. He moves closer.

A voice stops him.

The voice is weary, irritable. 'How many times have I told you. If you're going to play with the cargo at least have the decency to wait until I'm free to join in. Heaven only knows, there's precious little amusement in my life already, without you robbing me of whatever little I do have by killing someone while I'm not there to enjoy it.'

This is the moment you realise you will never reach Earth. Cindy will never see her mother. The kid will never claim a paycheck, company ratified or otherwise.

Instead you will all die, slowly and painfully, at the hands of Ass-face, his Cap'n and the rest of the jackers.

And there isn't a single thing you can do to prevent it.

– 2 –

The voice belongs to the Cap'n. His expression is

mild, but the voice itself is deeply resonant, with a metallic edge, as if a bandsaw was hard at work somewhere deep in the Cap'n's chest.

If you thought Ass-face looked ugly, he's a wet lace handkerchief compared to the Cap'n. The phrase *ugly as sin* springs to mind. The Cap'n is as ugly as all the sins he's ever committed. And if you believe the stories, he's crammed a lifetime of sins into the year he's been terrorising the spacelanes.

Now he's looking at you out of one human eye and one eye that's about as far from human as you can get.

The eye that is human is bruised and rheumy, the colour of nicotine stains. It is the eye of a rabid animal running one step this side of madness. The eye that isn't human is a demon's eye – a steel demon's eye – and it rides high in a steel demon's face.

Those terrible eyes fasten onto you with the patience of madness and you get a sudden vision of hammers rising and falling in the night, beating against steel and flesh and wedding them immutably together around the Cap'n's skull.

The face lurches still closer. It lurches because the Cap'n limps. Beneath his long leather coat one leg is stiff. It rings, metal on metal, as the Cap'n walks. And one shoulder, too, is lumpy, misshapen, the arm with it. Beneath the coat you can make out no details – but the hand that emerges from the specially-widened sleeve of the coat looks like it belongs more properly on a foundry waldo than a man. And it whirrs when he clenches his fist.

This, then, is Cap'n Macanudo.

The Mako.

Not a man but a devil. The devil that jacked Kev the Thief and sent back little more than a box of body parts to comfort his grieving friends and relatives. To the Cap'n it was a joke.

You wonder bleakly how he will amuse himself with you.

While he's looking from one of you to the other, obviously giving this matter his full attention, Ass-face mutters something about the cargo manifest.

'It says here they're hauling sex dolls.'

The Cap'n lets his gaze linger on Cindy. 'Really?'

Cindy sighs and casts a look of her own at Wankbreath, lying dead at her feet.

The Cap'n shrugs. 'A girl after my own heart. Ass-face, recycle the meat.'

At that moment the jacker whom Ass-face torched crawls out from between stacks of junk, face a weeping mask. 'Cap'n. Help. My face. Help me, please.'

The Cap'n considers the human wreckage at

his feet before finishing his sentence. 'As I said, recycle the meat. Both pieces.'

The corpse and the burned jacker are dragged off. Only one of them screams a protest.

The Cap'n now turns his entire attention to Cindy.

He thrusts his metal hand deep into a specially enlarged pocket. He strides towards her, metal foot crashing against the deck. He stops with his face a breath from hers.

She is motionless.

He blinks. His human eye moves slowly from side to side, taking in the planes and curves of her face, the texture of her skin.

The eye closes.

He inhales sharply.

Cindy jerks back until her head thumps against the gallows pole.

'You have been perspiring.'

Cindy blinks. Suspended beside her, Mike is going a little crazy. Ass-face holds the oxy-cutter close to his face. Mike shuts up.

'I assume it was hot in your rig.'

'Like, it was a hundred and seventy in the cab.'

With a sudden movement the Cap'n takes a monogrammed handkerchief from his pocket and mops Cindy's face with it. He does this gently, almost reverently. Then he holds the cloth to his nose and inhales again, deeply.

'I compliment you, my dear. You have a distinctive and not unpleasant body odour.'

Cindy blinks. She still has one hand free. You have a second to wonder what she might do with it, and what the reprisals might be, then your mouth is off on a little trip of its own again.

'Cap'n! Cap'n. We'd just like to take this opportunity to thank you for saving us.'

Mike picks up the strategy. 'Yeah. We're real grateful.'

The Cap'n looks from one of you to the other. When he laughs it is the sound of steel tearing. 'I didn't save you, you Company scumbags. I jacked your load.'

'Absolutely. Of course, whatever you say. We appreciate it. We truly do. But it's very important you understand that we don't work for the Company.'

'Oh?'

'Well, I mean. Have you ever seen Company drivers wearing nothing but their underwear while on duty?'

The Cap'n considers. He inhales; you hear the sound of pumps whirring. He blinks. Both eyes this time. One is silent, the other scrapes like a rusty camera iris. The human eye glances briefly at Mike's groin.

Mike begins to panic. You hope he can manage it silently.

159

The Cap'n says, 'I want to know what your cargo is, who's the skipper, and who's the consignee.'

Mike licks his lips. 'We don't know none of that.'

You groan inwardly.

The Cap'n drags the waiter's trolley closer. There's a hint of a smile in his voice as he says, conversationally, 'You're going to kick yourself later. Because if you had troubled to inform yourself –' the metal hand whips away the linen cloth from the trolley to reveal an array of surgical tools, small metalworking tools, a bandsaw and a welder's angle-grinder '– I wouldn't have to slice off your manly process.'

Mike bites his lip. His glance leaps from the tools to the Cap'n to you. 'Is he talking about my dick?'

You sigh. 'Cap'n, we're just independent contract haulers. We're trying to make a living and we don't ask a lot of questions. What we do know is whatever's in those trailers is not something you want to go messing with.'

The Cap'n clumps across to you and thrusts his demon's eye into your face. It scrapes shut then open in a rusty blink. You think you can see little sparks in there, like arcing electricity. 'Do I look like someone to mess with?' His voice hardens, bandsaws grind. 'Like I have the IQ of an egg-timer, perhaps?' A metallic thumb jerks towards *Betty*, partially hidden behind piles of junk. 'Those are high security double-z containers you're hauling there. I say the pair of you are Company butt-boys.'

Something snaps inside then. 'Cap'n Macanudo, I'm fifty-four years old. I been hauling trucks since before you were born. Which makes me pretty old, I guess, but I been around. And you can jack my load, and chain me to a gallows pole, and harass my girl, and threaten to cut off my partner's dick if that is your pleasure. But if you accuse me just once more of working for the goddamn lily-livered, butt-sucking Company, and I ever get free of these goddamn chains, I will personally rip out your one good eye and eat it for breakfast with toasted waffles and jam!'

You suck in a breath. It gives the Cap'n a chance to consider your words.

'And I tell you this: you can even hack my dick off – and I'll change my name to Terry or Lee or something else neutral like that – but it ain't gonna change what I know, and it ain't gonna change the facts: the only way you're gonna find out what's in those trailers is to cut 'em open and stick your goddamn head in there and take a goddamn look with that one good goddamn eye of yours.'

The Cap'n frowns.

'Now will you please get the hell out of my face? The sound of pumps hissing when you breath is making me claustrophobic.'

The Cap'n scowls. His eyes narrow angrily. He bites his lip: ceramic teeth click on moulded resin.

'John Canyon. You are a wild card. Too old to be scared, too far from death yet to be intimately acquainted with the fear that nearness brings.' The Cap'n seems to reach a decision. 'I am going to run the proof for Fourier's theorem in my head. This will take approximately one and a half minutes. Then we will begin again. In the mean time, forgive me if I think aloud. I do that sometimes when I am distracted, such as by contemplation of the many inventive deaths I could devise for yourself and your companions. Now. If you will excuse me?'

He turns away.

He looks once again at Cindy.

He mumbles. 'I was head of Company R. & D. Built the new toys. Dreamed them up too. A top man slotted for the big job. But I was betrayed by that bastard E.J. Saggs. Thought he'd killed me. Used the new toy. The fat-assed fool. His mistake was having it done in my own lab. I was able to recreate my body; my mind. I am the Phoenix. You have heard the name? The bird that burns?

That dies and lives again? I have died. I have known death and it is . . . it is . . . *boring*. There are no theorems when you are dead. No proofs to be found. No colleagues to ridicule. No advantages to be won. No ground to lose. It is boring. You know the one thing I have discovered since being reborn? The one great truth? I'll tell you. Nothing is as interesting as killing someone. Well, actually I lie. Sex is still pretty interesting. In fact candidly, I must admit to being somewhat obsessed by it. This may be because I haven't had any for some while. But then, of course, there's a reason for that.'

He pauses for a moment, his gaze lingering on Cindy. 'You are a very attractive woman. In the normal course of human affairs you probably wouldn't look twice at someone like myself. I am drawn to beauty like other men . . . ah, dearest beauty . . . she gives me a wide berth in life's halls – so to speak.' He pauses thoughtfully once again. 'So . . . were you not chained to a major support beam of my ship I wouldn't stand a chance of having sex with someone as alluring as yourself.'

His hands move then, one flesh, one not. Demon's hands. Hands that had removed intimate portions of Kev the Thief's body – among many, many others – move to caress the woman you plan to marry.

163

You're on the point of – well, what, exactly, you don't know; you are still chained up after all – when Mike gives vent to his prodigious storehouse of blasphemy. 'Leave her alone, you half electric asshole.'

You're talking at once. 'He didn't mean it. He respects the brave way you confront your disability.'

Until now the Cap'n has been running on automatic. Now he awakes. 'Kill them. Kill them both. Kill them now.'

His smile of anticipation is terrifying.

Mike begins a new protest. Ass-face comes closer with the oxy-cutter.

The only person not affected is Cindy herself. 'You're threatening to rape me. You think that's, like, the worst thing you could do to me? I got to get to Earth. I got to see my mother. Keep the load. Give us the rig and promise to let us go and – I'll have sex with you.'

Her words stop the Cap'n in his tracks. They stop Ass-face's oxy-cutter a hand's breadth from Mike's face.

They stop your heart in your chest.

'Christ, Cindy, I'm fifty-four years old. You trying to give me a heart attack? Don't say things like that.'

The Cap'n ignores you. His expression is unreadable. 'You would have sex with me?'

Cindy agrees. 'Right here on the deck if I have to.'

The Cap'n nods thoughtfully. He holds out a hand and Ass-face drops the keys to the manacles into it.

He unlocks Cindy.

She rubs her wrists. Her expression is unreadable.

'Then shall we retire to my quarters?'

'If that's what it takes. But you must promise to free my friends.'

'If that's what it takes.'

And he leads her away. Just like that.

Mike's expression is indescribable. *We've got to do something*!

'Don't co-opt the right to be indignant, Mike. She's my fiancée.'

Bare-Assed Scum

– 1 –

He takes you through seventeen decks – you count them – to the bows of the *Regalia*. After thirty minutes' walking you forget how many staterooms and cabins and gym halls and swimming pools you pass, all of them piled high with jacked loot. Your bare feet ache from the hurried pace and the occasional item of loose trash the jackers have left on the deck.

Also, whatever else they might be, the jackers are not very clean. Grease and moisture coats the walls and trickles to the deck. As you get further towards the core of the ship the gravity eases off, and the moisture spreads. The smell of rust and mould gets stronger.

You say nothing. What's the point?

Finally you emerge from an executive elevator into the main concourse. This is as wide as three streets; and must once have been very beautiful.

Fake-sandstone cladding lines the walls. Shops vanish into the distance in both directions. Fake-stone pillars separate the shop fronts and form cloistered areas at intervals along the concourse.

At various places ornamental bushes have run wild, exploding from the large pots and sending roots and branches exploring throughout the guts of the ship.

As you look further along the concourse, you see the overhead lights are damaged – probably scavenged over the years for the operational areas of the ship. Several ranks of shops are in semi-darkness.

Somewhere a dog howls.

There is broken glass everywhere, from the shattered windows.

The Cap'n notes the glass, studies your feet for a moment, then reaches into a nearby shop and extracts a pair of sandals, which he hands to you.

Feeling an unexpected gratitude, you put them on.

'My dear, I think before we retire to my state-rooms for our carnal indulgences, we will go shopping.'

He leads the way through the boulevard. Every few shops, he hesitates. At one he punches out the remaining glass from the window and ushers you in.

'This boulevard is five miles long. Ten miles of shopping fronts for your consumer pleasure. I think we can find some suitable boudoir attire for you here. Do you not agree?'

You say nothing. No wonder there were no

rich people left on Earth. They probably all lived here on the *Regalia* – before it was jacked.

He gestures to the many items of clothing still on display here. You stare around in dumb surprise.

'Nothing catch your fancy? Never mind. We will continue. It's my experience that the *Regalia* has something for everyone.'

After a while the boulevard walk becomes disorientating. In less than twenty minutes the Cap'n has presented you with more of the most exciting, expensive dresses than you have ever dreamed of, let alone seen. Silk, lace, leather, latex. Saris and cocktail dresses, morning wear, evening wear, casual wear, sports wear. There seems no end to it.

You are not surprised to notice that all of it is leisure wear.

Your mind is buzzing with it. You feel dizzy. The experience is surreal, not entirely unpleasant, yet dredged with the knowledge of why he is doing this, what he will do to you, what he might already have done to Mike and John.

Finally the Cap'n pauses before a long, expensively appointed shop-front. The gilt sign above the window reads simply:

Harrods of Knightsbridge

He stands captivated before the most luscious dress you have ever seen. It is full and tight in all the right places, pale cream with a pearly sheen that is offset by what looks like – but probably isn't – about a hundredweight of peach silk.

It is lit by shafts of light coming through holes where the ceiling has been torn apart by blaster-fire. The thinnest splash of blood runs across the bodice and beneath one sleeve, testament to a jacked passenger, or perhaps a shop manager attempting a last ditch defence of their property.

The brown splash contrasts perfectly with the silk.

The moment is beautiful and terrible all at once; dreamlike, surreal, yet utterly captivating.

The Cap'n notices your expression. 'Perfect,' he breathes. Even the whine of pumps in his chest is subdued. 'Absolutely perfect.'

'I've never seen anything so beautiful. It is a . . . ballgown?'

'My dear, it is that very thing. And the fact that you stumbled over the word is enchanting. As enchanting as I am sure you will look in the dress when you wear it for me.'

You bite your lip. Suddenly whatever pleasure the moment held is gone.

The Cap'n reaches for the dress, and the shoes beside it. Then he stops. As if realising a certain reverence is required, he stubs out his cigar and reaches in again. Servos whine in his arm as he takes them tenderly from their stand.

He offers them to you.

You take them from him. The dress feels wonderful; cool against your burning skin. But you can't keep it. Not yet. You hand the dress back to him. It's hard to let it go.

His expression is a mixture of anger and confusion.

You tell him why. 'Man, I have been shot up and roasted alive and tortured by your goddam thugs. I stink and I gotta use the ladies' room. And I need a shower.'

'Oh.' He thinks the matter over, assessing the level of threat you possess, what tricks you might play, how pleasant your body odour is. 'If you think that is necessary. By all means.'

You wash – bathe might be a better word – in a luxury swimming pool the size of a tennis court. The water is the perfect temperature; constantly recycled by machinery the jackers had found no need for. You wonder why they don't keep themselves cleaner if it is this easy to access water. You get your answer when the Cap'n locks the bulkhead when you're inside.

He watches you undress in the changing rooms but won't follow you into the pool.

'You don't want to watch?'

'Parts of me have a problem with water. As

170

you may imagine.'

You wonder then why he has a key to the pool. The answer comes as you towel yourself dry. Perhaps the Cap'n can disconnect his artificial limbs. He'd have to stay clean somehow. Perhaps he comes here once a day – week, month – and indulges in a one-legged, one-armed swim. Of course he'd be very vulnerable to attack at this time, from jealous jackers with designs on the Captaincy. He'd have to ensure against that. Hence the key and the steel bulkhead.

You file the knowledge away for whatever use it may be later.

After the shower he watches you dress in the ballgown, tightens the corset and bows around you himself with delicate whirrings of metal fingers. He has lit up another cigar by now – but it's a quality brand. The aroma is faintly attractive. And of course – he doesn't have to worry about what the nicotine is doing to his lungs, because judging by the hiss of pumps when he breathes, he probably doesn't have any.

When you are dressed he takes you forward, right up to the bows of the ship. To the ballroom.

The ballroom is a low-g area: a cylinder counterspun to offset the centripetal force of the rest of the passenger country. It is big enough to hold a sizeable portion of the *Regalia*'s full complement of passengers and officers – when she had any passengers and officers. It is gorgeously appointed. Crystal chandeliers are suspended from the cylinder core. There are gilt-edged glass tables and chairs. Deep pile rugs line the cylinders. The end wall through which you enter is a bar constructed of oak panelling and green baize and gilded mirrors. In it is reflected the opposite end wall – a domed expanse of glass which looks directly out into the big dark.

Stars curve past the dome, together with the odd streaky reflection from black rock. Every so often there is a colourful flash as a chunk that wanders too close to the *Regalia* is vaporised by the meteor defence system.

You stand in awe, entranced by the beauty of the room.

The Cap'n moves to the bar, strangely graceful in the low gravity, reaches into a wooden panel and suddenly the air is filled with music. Violins. Cellos. Piccolos. Flutes. Instruments you have no names for and others you have never heard.

'Mendelssohn. Beautiful, is it not?'

You are devastated.

For a while he stands watching you listening to the music. You realise you are crying when he gently wipes a tear from your cheek. After a while he takes your hand in his, the human one, and asks you if you would care to dance.

You stare at his ravaged face, the bruised flesh,

the beaten metal components of his skull. The demon's eye. You know he has killed men. Many men. Jacked their loads and ended their lives in terrible ways. He has said as much himself. You cannot imagine how much hate and fear and self-loathing and self-pity he must hold inside. And yet he is calm. Almost rational. And intelligent. Some part of you knows he is seducing you. That it's all part of the game. But all this . . . it's so beautiful, so . . . unexpected. Surely it can't hurt just to play along – for a while anyway?

'I can't . . . I mean, I don't know how. I've never danced – not properly. I mean we had barn-dances in the cargo deck on SkyTown but they were nothing like . . .' You don't have the words to describe your feelings so you fall silent instead.

'I understand. A ship such as this . . . a man such as myself for company . . . all outside the life experience of – what are you? – a burger bar waitress?' Without waiting for a reply he continues. 'But you are young. You can learn. I will teach you how.'

'But John . . . and Mike . . .'

'You have my promise that they will be safe . . . as long as you keep your promise.'

You think about that for a moment.

When he asks again if you wish to dance, it is the easiest thing in the world to say yes.

2

You rub the mirrorglass plate where your nose used to be and study the line of cargo trailers backwards from Canyon's rig.

What's in those trailers? Gold? Jewels? Electronics? Art? High value stuff or worthless crap?

Time was when you'd have been able to sniff out the contents from a hundred yards. They didn't call you the Nose for nothing. Now, of course, they call you the same name for a different reason. Now they call you that not because you have a skilful one, but because you don't have one at all. One day it's gonna stop. The bullying, the piss-taking. You're determined about that.

You're right too. It's going to stop, and real soon. But not for the reason you think.

It's a joke to them, to Ass-face, the guy that took away your nose. Anyone else and they'd be paranoid about revenge; that one night you might sneak up to them as they slept and use a bread knife to remove more than just their nose. But oh no, not Ass-Face. The man has no respect. No respect for anyone or anything, let alone for you, who were once the hottest cargo-sniffer in the business.

A slow voice at your side says, 'Nose, I know that look on your face. The reason you lost that nose is 'cause you shoved it into someone else's business.'

You don't look round. The voice belongs to Rings. He's marking time to an unheard beat. His fat belly wobbles and all the rings on him jingle in time with his pumping foot. He's a very musical guy. He's your best mate. Your only real mate, actually. He's the only one you'll take that kind of crap from.

And Rings knows it. 'So if you're getting depressed take your damn medication. We've got a job to do.'

And that is sussing out what's in the trailers.

You unship the portable scanner. As a matter of fact, the scanner isn't actually that portable – it rides an infirmary gurney, unused since the jacking of the *Regalia* for its intended purpose of helping to save lives. You attach the sensors to the lock of the first cargo trailer and punch up a readout.

Nothing.

You kick the scanner.

Still nothing.

'What's the matter with the damn thing? Batteries flat?'

You kick it again.

Rings says, 'Go easy on the machine, man.'

'If I still had my nose we wouldn't need the damn machine.'

Rings sighs. 'I hate circular conversations. Get the chisel.'

The chisel is tungsten alloy and is attached to an industrial-rated hydraulic ram. It can punch a hole in these trailers fast as blinking. You clamp the chisel to the lock, fire up the ram and stand clear. The chisel fires, there is an almighty crack and bits of metal shrapnel shoot across the cargo deck, raising shouts of protest from upwards of a hundred yards away.

Ignoring the shouts, you grin at Rings and take away the chisel. You expect to see the lock shattered, a fist-sized hole where it had been.

The cargo trailer isn't scratched. 'I don't get it.'

Rings is holding up the chisel. The blade has sheared off some six inches from the ram. 'It's the chisel, man. We bust the chisel.'

'Jeez.'

Rings shrugs. 'Alright then, if the chisel's no good, let's try –'

Before Rings can finish his sentence, there is a metallic whirring sound. Hatches open in the cargo trailer and two guns emerge.

You stare at them. 'Jeez fuck a shit souffle –'

The guns open fire with perfect timing. You dive to the floor, hit rolling, body numb with the impact. Dimly you are aware of Rings yelling, the sound of blaster fire. The trailer guns rake the cargo deck with laser light, visible only as faint scratches in the air where the beams pass through smoke, or metal or flesh.

You stay down. Your chest hurts. You must have cracked a rib. Rings cries out again.

Hey rings, you OK, man? The words come out as a gasp. Or maybe they don't come out at all.

There's more gunfire, more yelling, an explosion, then another.

Then silence.

Rings appears. You struggled to sit up but can't make it.

Rings, man, you OK? I thought you was a gonna! What the fuck was that?

Rings doesn't seem to hear you. He is looking at you with a peculiar expression. He wrinkles his nose, as if he smells something bad. The last time he made an expression like that was when Eddie the Feeler cooked his arm on a live power feed he was trying to fix.

Hey Rings, man. What's cooking?

Ring's doesn't reply. It's as if he doesn't hear you.

He looks at your stomach.

You follow his gaze.

The last thing you see is a ragged hole the size of a dinner plate melted through your coveralls. It's melted through your stomach too. The edges of the hole are blackened. Smoke is rising from cauterised flash.

Rings was right: something is cooking.

It's you.

– 3 –

The dance is over.

The music reaches a crescendo and slams to a halt. The Cap'n whirls you to one end of the ballroom, places you gently on deep pile carpet and smiles. He bows from the waist and his hips make a peculiar mechanical whirring sound.

'Thank you, my dear. That was entrancing. And now, I think, to business.'

You get a cold feeling in your gut. You know what business he means.

He takes you by the hand, a gentle but unavoidable grasp, and leads you from the ballroom. His boudoir is only a short distance away. It is a full suite, obviously once intended for very important passengers – maybe even royalty.

A huge canopied bed dominates the room. There is a bar. Actually there are two bars. One contains bottles of alcohol, mixers, glasses, and the other contains about a hundred glass phials full of coloured powders and pills, together with boxes of plastic sachets containing syringes. In addition, the room is piled high with jacked loot. Jewellery, clothing, art, electronics. The Cap'n is evidently a man who likes to gloat over his conquests, both material and . . . otherwise.

He leads you to the bed and sits you down. He then crosses to the twin bars. 'What would make you more comfortable, my dear? I have seven different forms of sedation. Alcohol, the usual pharmacology . . . the unusual pharmacology . . .'

You bite your lip. 'Let's not fool ourselves, Cap'n. The dance was nice. The dress is lovely, but I can't be bought and I don't like toys. I volunteered for this job so let's get on with it, shall we?'

'So it's a job now, is it?'

You can't think of a thing to say in reply. You begin to undress instead. He watches you. He doesn't tell you to do it faster or slower. He doesn't tell you what he wants, what he likes. He doesn't ask you what you like. He doesn't speak at all. He just watches. And now his one human eye is beginning to look disturbingly like his demon's eye. Unblinking. Obsessive.

You unlace the corset. Kick off your shoes. Peel away the bodice.

You slip out of the gown.

You stand, naked, and wait.

He waits too; he's just drinking you in. Every curve and angle, every hair and limb and look. Every movement.

Then with a sudden, smooth movement, he takes off his coat and drapes it over a nearby Regency chair.

You can't help staring.

His chest is heavily scarred, split along the breastbone, skin seamed to fit the beaten metal and plastic prosthesis which forms the left half of his body. Transparent access panels glimmer with internal light. The light flickers as whirring fans cool machine components. His human arm is strong, the muscle tone good beneath scarred flesh. Yet it looks almost feeble in comparison to the bulk of his mechanical arm.

Another movement and his trousers are gone.

Well. You knew that was coming.

The half-man-half-machine motif continues through his hips and buttocks, down into his left leg, which is built around a massive hydraulic ram and ends in a steel peg and ball.

You try to avoid thinking about what lies between his thighs and his stomach. That becomes problematical when he pulls the starter cord and it hums to life.

'I rebuilt everything,' he says proudly. 'Every organ. And in respect of our mutual unfinished business, I now emit a low-amp electrical pulse designed to drive women wild with pleasure.'

OK. Fine. That's it. You've had enough. 'You're gonna make me puke! You keep talking and this deal is off.'

The Cap'n moves towards you, takes you by the arms and places you on the bed. He's about to move closer when the humming falters and dies. He looks downwards. The look of embarrassment on his face is almost comical.

Apparently he rebuilt his ego too.

You sigh inwardly with relief. 'Never mind, Cap'n. That sort of thing happens to everyone sometimes.'

'Not to me. I'm not programmed for it.'

He wrenches at the starter cord. Motors hum and circuits click. Nothing else happens. Now concern – and some degree of panic – joins the embarrassment on the human half of his face. The demon's eye iris shuts as if attempting to analyse and resolve the problem all by itself.

His voice shakes with self-consciousness. 'I pray you allow me a few moments to co-ordinate my seldom used reproductive sequences.'

You shrug. 'Oh sure, honey. Why don't I make us a drink while you're . . . er . . . you know, trying to get the old motor started?'

'An excellent suggestion, my dear. There's –' a jerk on the cord; an aborted whirr – 'champagne in the cooler. Why don't you grab – ' another. And another – 'a couple of . . . you know . . . glasses.'

You cross to the bar. The champagne is hard to miss. There are at least thirty bottles of it behind the bar. Bollinger. Different years. You grab the nearest one. And a bucket of ice.

You swirl the ice, thinking of the pool, your conversation there.

Parts of me have a problem with water.

At that moment the Cap'n gives a triumphant groan. His latest attempt to jump-start himself has succeeded. Now, in addition to the usual activity there is a pretty blue glow as well.

'There we are, my dear. One hundred per cent operational at last.'

He turns to show you – and you thrust the bucket of ice into his groin. 'Oh my God, I'm so sorry, I tripped, I hope I haven't damaged your –'

He cuts you off with an agonised groan and crashes to the carpeted deck, where he proceeds to enter what could only be described as a demented fit.

You fall silent. The Cap'n is lying on the floor, limbs thrashing, semi-conscious, electrical short circuits spreading from his groin throughout his body. His flesh is beginning to scorch lightly in one or two places. Half a skull full of hair stands completely on end. His human eye rolls back in its socket – the other iris opens and shuts with manic speed. His body continues to thrash violently. A couple of plugs come loose in a shower of fluid. Oil? Blood?

Jeez. Your plan was to stop him fucking you, not kill him.

What the hell: every cloud has a silver lining.

Without pausing for thought, you grab his coat off the chair, clean trousers and a peaked cap from the house-sized wardrobe, and his boot from where he dropped it on the floor. Then you're out of the door and running madly through the ship.

– 4 –

Back in the cargo deck, life hasn't changed much. You're still chained to the gallows pole. Mike is still making a fuss. Ass-face is still looking to tenderise your nuts with his damn oxy-cutter.

Mike has been wittering on for some time now – almost as long as Cindy's been gone. He only stopped once and that was in order to try to dodge blaster ricochets from the trailer guns when they fried Nose as well. His voice has become a weary drone. Even Ass-face looks bored.

'John. We gotta do something. We gotta do it now. You know what's happening to her up there? What he's doing to her? John? Are you listening to me, man? You hear what I'm saying?'

'It's not the first time, kid, and she's doing it for the team.' You try to keep your voice expressionless. That way you don't have to think about what is really going on up there. You suspect it may be far worse than just sex. And if it is, there's absolutely nothing you can do about it.

Not while you're chained up anyway.

Mike swears at you.

You shrug, insofar as you can shrug while chained to a post.

'You chickenshit, John. She's your goddam fiancée. Don't you care what's happening to her?'

You sigh. 'Hey, Ass-face. Get this damn kid away from me willya? He's raising my blood pressure.'

Ass-face leans against a nearby pile of scrap and grins. 'Think I'd fall for that line? You got a great sense of humour, Canyon. Believe me you gonna need it. And soon.'

And Mike's off again. Don't you turn away from me, Canyon. We're just gonna hang here while Cindy's getting raped up there?'

Jeez, Mike. Quit chattering about it and do something!

You rattle your chains. 'You got a better plan, kid?'

'Sure I got a better plan.' Abruptly he swings his legs into the air and locks them around your neck. 'It's your goddam fault we're here. Now you can pay!' he squeezes. Hard. You start to choke.

This is more like it.

After a moment your struggles ceases and you let your body slump.

Ass-face sighs. 'Now look what you've done,

kid. You're gonna wish you hadn't made me stop you doing that.' He holds the cutter casually up to Mike's ankles. Mike screeches and falls away. Ass-face lifts the cutter towards Mike's face – and that's when you hit him with a donkey kick in the only part of him within reach – his ass.

It doesn't hurt him but it knocks him off balance – enough so that Mike can fetch him a good one in the groin. He falls over backwards – and you finish the job with another kick – this time to the head. He struggles to stand. For a moment it looks as though he'll make it. Then he collapses with a sigh on to the oxy-cutter.

His shirt starts to burn.

You use your feet to pull him slightly towards you.

'Hurry up before the smell brings someone.'

'Jeez, Mike, did you have to strangle me so hard?'

'Quit complaining. It had to look real, didn't it?'

'Yeah. It looked real because it was real. One more minute and I'd have been unconscious and then where would you have been, eh? Ah!'

Your exploring toes have grasped the key loosely tethered to Ass-face's belt. You slip them off the catch. You try to flip them to Mike.

The smoke rising from Ass-face's body makes you cough.

The keys slip from your grasp.

'Jeez, John, be careful. Lose them and we're dead.'

'I ain't no monkey, man.' You immediately prove yourself wrong by getting a perfect grip on the keys and flipping them into the air by Mike's head.

He grabs for them. 'Gottem!'

'Don't shout about it. Use 'em!'

But it's too late.

Ass-face groans, stirs, leaps to his feat with a squeal of pain, finds a bucket of slop and tips it over himself to put out the flames licking at his shirt and chest.

'Jeez. I'm gonna kill you fuckers. I'm gonna kill you so slowly you'll think it's a career.'

He picks up the oxy-cutter. The flame is still bright.

He moves towards you.

At that moment a familiar figure limps towards you from between piles of scrap.

Ass-face turns. 'Cap'n!'

The figure limps closer, points at the trolley-load of medical instruments and power tools.

You stare at the figure. It seems awful small for the Cap'n. 'You're back awful quick. She ride you out?'

The figure snaps its fingers at Ass-face.

He grins. 'You want me to kill 'em?'

A shake of the head.

'You want to kill 'em yourself?'

A nod.

'Well, that's a shame –' Ass-face abruptly rips the cap off Cindy's head – 'considering how they're your friends an' all.'

'Shit.'

At that moment another figure appears from between piles of junk. The real Cap'n. He's wearing a bathrobe and carrying a screwdriver. Behind him are a number of jackers, including Rings. They've all got guns. They're all pointed at you.

Cindy sighs. 'Shit. You really are a regular Mister Fixit.'

He stumps closer and rips off the coat she is wearing. He puts it on. He takes his cap from Ass-face.

'I'm sorry you couldn't find it in your heart to give me a chance, my dear. You could have been my beloved concubine and shared in my position here.'

'Guess that wasn't in my fortune cookie.'

He shrugs. 'Now all you'll share is my crew. Three hundred and ten of them in random order.' He takes the cutter from Ass-face and uses it to light a cigar. 'But first you can watch me kill your friends.' He sucks on a cigar, blows smoke into your face. 'Or, if you prefer, you can scrunch up your cute little nose and turn the other way.'

– 5 –

That's when, in the words of the immortal Mister Wells, "The heat ray spoke again, and this time it sent them to oblivion."

Well, it sends half a dozen jackers, two piles of worthless scrap and a fleeing cow to oblivion, anyway.

But not the Cap'n, more's the pity.

He just stands, turning slowly to peruse this new interruption to your gleefully anticipated death. Beams of laser light split the air around him until it looks like a smoky, shattered mirror. Explosions and screams echo throughout the cargo deck. Another cow squeals in fright. Someone's missed dinner. Not that anyone's worried about that now. They're all too busy dodging the attack.

You crane your neck and just manage to peep around the corner of a pile of junk. The guns have emerged from the second trailer and are firing to repel what they obviously perceive to be a continuing attack on the first. That is to say, they are firing at some jackers who have placed a thermite device against the hull, set the detonator and who are now running like all the demons of hell are after them.

They wouldn't be far wrong at that.

The beams are being deflected by piles of junk the jackers are running between. The beams are leaping and cavorting all over the cargo deck, for all the world like demons themselves, turning junk and priceless cargo and jackers and cows alike into worthless scrap.

Then the thermite device goes off with an almighty thump. Chunks of metal trailing smoke shoot across the deck. It's a repeat of Nose's and Ring's last effort, but with more success. This time the hot metal fragments are from the trailer itself.

It doesn't stop the guns firing though.

You crane your neck further. A five-foot hole has been blown in the side of the trailer. Smoke fills the hole. Beyond the smoke is darkness, lit occasionally by a flickering blue glare. Electrical short? More defence systems coming online?

No way to tell from here.

The Cap'n sees all this as well. Something about the trailer has caught his attention. He turns fully away from you towards the trailer. Dragging Cindy by one arm, he limps closer, the human half of his face distracted by inner thoughts, the demon's half focusing its complete attention on the target ahead. Laser beams split the air all around him. One tugs a strip away from the shoulder of his coat. Another blasts a six-inch hole in a scrap bin level with his head.

He treats the beams and the screams of dying men and the rattle and thump of weapons fire with equal regard – that is to say, none at all.

You'd have to say he has the luck of the devil because the last gun turret explodes under a barrage of blaster fire at the precise moment it targets him directly.

He wanders distractedly off to investigate, drawing Cindy along with him by the arm.

You breathe a sigh of relief. That cargo may have jetted right out of the mouth of hell but it just saved your life.

For the time being anyway.

Then the Cap'n's back and, judging by the look on his face, you wish you hadn't looked that particular gift horse in the mouth.

'I suppose you'll have guessed by now that I'm a mite curious about that's in those trailers, seeing as how it's already killed several of my crew. And seeing as how you claim not to know what you're carrying, I thought I'd postpone your deaths in favour of a little education. Now ain't that generous of me?' He sucks on his cigar, blows smoke into your face, jerks the cigar at the trailers. 'Get in there and find out what you're carrying. Get out alive, tell me what's in there, and I might just let you and the girl go free. Ladies and gentlemen, that's the deal on the table. Whaddya say?'

Sex Dolls

In the death – which is what his actions will mean for everyone aboard the *Regalia* – the Cap'n cannot resist taking a few men and following you into the trailer.

It's dark in here.

Well, not entirely dark.

There are little blips of light, tiny reflections from thick tubes coursing with glutinous liquid. Some of the light is red, some blue. It looks uncomfortably like veinous and arterial blood. The inside of the trailer is a nest of these snaking tubes, some thin as a finger, some as thick as your leg. You stand in the opening caused by the jackers' explosive charge and peer further inside. You cannot see much. You take a step forward. Your boot slips on brown fluid – many of the nearest tubes have been damaged by the blast which opened the trailer. You grab a hand-ful of tubes to keep your balance. The tubes sway, smack together with a glutinous sound, but hold firm. In the opening behind them is revealed a number of plastic sacks. Like the

191

tubes these too are semi-transparent, fluid filled. Inside are dark, irregular shapes. Organs? If the fluid in the tubes is blood that might not be so far from the truth.

Are the trailers full of medical supplies? Donor organs and body fluids intended for use on Earth?

If so, why defend them with smartguns the military would fall over themselves to possess?

What if it's medical supplies for troops – an army that someone intends to use on Earth?

Why use an army on Earth? OK, ninety per cent of the population is deemed surplus to requirements by unofficial sources. But still . . .

You get a sick feeling then.

The feeling intensifies as the Cap'n waves his gun by way of suggesting you move deeper into the trailer.

The damaged area of tubing falls behind you as you move further into the trailer. Your footing improves as you pass beyond the flooded areas of deck. You force a path between the ubiquitous tubes, stepping over and ducking under them where necessary. Now that you're in among them you can hear them gurgling as the fluid inside flows sluggishly from one part of the trailer to another.

And there's another sound. A kind of pulse. Like a heartbeat.

But not a human heartbeat.

Mike's voice breaks the silence – abrupt and almost too normal-sounding in this alien environment. 'This is number one weird.'

You tell him to shut up. You're hearing something else now, something that's scaring the wits out of you. It wavers on the edge of hearing, distant, echoing through the depths of the trailer, partially masked by glutinous drippings and gurglings.

It's the sound of babies screaming.

But not human babies.

'Holy shit, what is this junk? What's that sound? What's *that*? Oh man, is that what I think it is?'

Once again you tell Mike to shut the hell up. You have an answer now and it's an answer straight out of the fiery jaws of hell.

The Cap'n knows it too.

'It's my babies. It's my new toys.'

Mike shoots you a look that is barely distinguishable in the two-tone gloom. You nod. Mike's right. The Cap'n is losing it, big time.

The Cap'n pushes his way past you now, gun pointing at the floor. Lost in some half-remembered past, he's forgotten all about you.

Mike tugs your arm. 'Let's get the hell out.'

Jackers' guns at your back remind you the choice would be imprudent.

'Besides, I got a hankering to see what the hell we're supposed to be carrying.'

'Jeez, Canyon, you got a death wish or something?'

You shrug. 'If I'm gonna die I at least want to know what the hell is trying to kill me.'

'John Canyon, you're a dyed in the wool, prime-cut, grade-A asshole, you know that?'

'Well, Mister Puccini. Call a spade a spade, why don't ya?'

'I told you before. My name's not –'

The Cap'n's back with you then, calling in a voice partially obscured by mutterings and grumblings and ratchety clicks and electronic squeaks issuing from the trailer junk. 'Get up here, now. I want you all to see this.'

When you see what he's looking at you get a bad feeling in the pit of your stomach to add to all the rest.

At first glance they resemble canned offal. But canned offal doesn't scream gently to itself – and twitch every now and then, as if it's having a really bad nightmare.

They're hanging in rows like slabs of hog bound up in Teflon and aluminium and glass wire. Wet lenses irised shut, limbs folded around steel cores, semisolid fluids sloshing gently in glass sacs. They're both animate and inanimate. Alive and dead.

194

Machines.

Embryos.

The Cap'n's new toys.

'Jeez, you ever see anything more likely to make you puke on your boots?'

'Mike, I told you to shut up.'

The Cap'n is already answering the question on everyone's lips. 'They're state-of-the-art killers. One of these'll vaporise a man in five hundred milliseconds and leave his wristwatch and pocket change on the deck.' The Cap'n is caressing the embryos now, running his hands across the damp organic surfaces, the slick metallic frames, his own body a mirror to theirs, a father in more senses than one. 'These babies are smart-weapons elevated to the wetware equivalent of godhood. They were E.J. Saggs' new toys. Now they're my new toys.'

He stops beside an empty hanger.

'All except this one.' He licks his lips. You watch the expression on his face closely. The Cap'n made these little beauties, did he? And now he's scared, is he?

The Cap'n begins to murmur quietly to himself. An old good luck charm, maybe. Perhaps he's finally tipped over the edge into complete madness. 'This little piggy went to market . . .'

You signal Mike and then begin backing away, slowly, so as not to arouse suspicion.

'. . . this little piggy stayed at home . . .'

There's no danger of that. The jackers' attentions are firmly fixed on the Cap'n, and his is fixed on the empty space where one of the new toys recently hung.

'. . . this little piggy had roast hog for dinner . . .'

He blinks. He takes a small device from a chain around his neck and holds it like a charm, a protection against the darkness to accompany his child's rhyme.

'. . . and this . . .'

He takes a step away from the empty space.

'. . . little piggy . . .'

The tubes beside him wave suddenly, branches in a breeze. Except there is no breeze. Not here, not in the trailer. No breeze that isn't made by –

The new toy is big – but not bulky. Its outline is hard to make out in the darkness because light seems to flow into it instead of being reflected from it. But it looks fast. And nasty. It towers over even the Cap'n's rebuilt frame. It reaches out for him gently, almost caressingly.

'. . . had none.'

The Cap'n aims his charm at the new toy and presses a button.

The toy freezes into immobility.

The Cap'n smiles confidently. '. . . this little piggy . . .'

The second new toy steps out from the shadows and stares at its maker.

The Cap'n's grin fades. '. . . this little piggy says, "Oh Shit."'

He tries to get the charm pointed at the new-comer. He's way too slow. The toy's eyes open wide and the child's nonsense rhyme dissolves into a scream. There is light: a momentary flash. Flesh sizzles. You hear a body fall – two bodies; the new toy has cut the Cap'n clean in half. The stink of charred flesh makes you want to puke. Instead you grab Mike by the arm and shove him back towards the opening in the trailer hull.

You're not surprised.

Somewhere along the line, running like a bastard from someone or something that wants to kill you seems to have become a habit.

– 2 –

The new toy follows you through the trailer. You can't hear it moving – it seems to absorb sound in the same way it absorbs light – but you know it's coming after you. You're no rocket scientist but your own eyes, coupled with what the Cap'n said about it before it sliced him in half, are enough to convince you it means no good.

And that in particular it means no good to *you*.

You are aware of movement all around as you force a way through the jungle of tubes. The gurglings are louder, the fluid moving faster within the tubes. And there is movement not directly related to your own.

Are more of these things waking up?

A scream cuts the thick air from behind as a jacker meets an untimely end. The scream ends in a kind of sizzling noise, like the sound hog steaks make cooking on a griddle.

You burst from the trailer with Mike in tow, to face a ring of hostile jackers, guns levelled.

Ass-face is at their head. 'What have you done with the Cap'n?'

You shrug, gibber something and fling yourself flat on the deck. Mike follows suit. Actually, he flings himself at Cindy, who is standing beside Ass-face. The jackers are taken somewhat by surprise by this apparent suicidal course of action. They all turn their guns on you or Mike – consequently leaving themselves open to attack by the toy when it comes out of the trailer.

Which, of course, is exactly what it does.

Rings is the first jacker to be targeted by the new toy. He swings a huge automatic at the toy and lets fly with an enormous salvo. Ignoring the gunfire, the toy plucks a single bullet from the air. It turns the bullet over in its hand, as if examining it. It tilts its head to one side as if considering. Then it drops the bullet and winks at Rings.

The eyes flash.

Rings dies with an unbelieving expression plastered across his face. His body shreds into vapour – fifty milliseconds per pound – leaving just his rings and other body ornamentation to clatter to the deck with a sound like the bursting of a bag of pirate doubloons.

By now the other jackers have rallied. Fifteen of them turn and spray the toy with bullets.

The toy shrugs off the hot steel as if it were a light shower of rain. Bullets ricochet across the cargo deck. Jackers dive for cover. A cow squeals in outrage as its legs are cut from beneath it. For a moment the toy is attracted by the body mass of the cow as it thumps into the deck. It targets the animal – then turns its attention back to the jackers. You watch all this from the marginal cover provided by a huge crate of machine parts. The Cap'n was right about their intelligence. Unlike the trailer guns, the new toy can tell the difference between a human and a cow. You guess that makes it at least as smart as the jackers it is killing.

The toy vaporises half a dozen jackers with a flip of its head. It moves fast, like a stallion with a mane of fire, tossing this way and that, pawing the air with three-foot blades which unfold from its upper limbs, kicking with alloy-clawed feet, vaporising with its baleful, triple-lensed glare. Jackers puff into vapour with agonised squeals, leaving a clutter of steaming metal components such as belt buckles, boot snaps, combs and assorted weaponry to clatter to the deck.

Ass-face is caught at the periphery of the blast and manages to crawl away. The heat of a nearby plasma burst ignites the ammunition belts slung over his shoulder and wrapped around his waist. He has a moment to register his fate before he is ripped into three distinct chunks by the simultaneous explosion of all three belts.

You look around for Mike and Cindy. They're nowhere in sight. Of course, they wouldn't be if they'd been vaporised. You watch the toy stamp lightly on the hand of a jacker faking death. The jacker screams and is cut in half. Another approaches the toy from behind, holding a heavy fire-axe above his head. The toy impales him without so much as a second glance. The axe falls from nerveless fingers and finishes the job.

Another jacker emerges from the freight eleva-tor. 'Suck on this, big boy!' he screams and hurls the biggest hand grenade you have ever seen directly at the toy. The toy catches the grenade, returns the pitch with sufficient force to push the jacker back into the freight elevator. He lands on the deck winded, has just enough time to notice the grenade rolling between his splayed legs before the doors close and you lose sight of him. Then the grenade explodes and you regain sight of him again – well, the various bits of him any-way – which explode through the shattered doors.

Worse is to come. The explosion crumples the elevator shaft, sending a heavy cargo-mover top-pling from its mount to explode amongst the gut-ted shells of a nearby jacked load.

Fire sirens cut loose across the deck. Foam spreads from emergency points, engulfing a posse of jackers who are loading their weapons with fresh ammunition. You take a moment to grin. It's probably the first bath any of them have had in months.

Fuel ignites in a nearby workshop. The shed explodes. A jacker is impaled by an airborne power drill. Another is simultaneously crushed and incinerated by a burning cylinder of cutting gas. You duck to avoid the rest of the power tools as they hurtle past in a deadly shower.

Flame and smoke spread across the cargo deck. If any one of those jacked rigs still has fuel in it you're all finished.

Jackers run through the smoke in crazy pat-terns. The explosions multiply. So do the sirens. You hear gunfire, screaming, the mooing of cows.

A hand touches your shoulder.

You turn fast, fist cocked to deliver a blow.

'So that's how you'd treat me if we were mar-ried?'

'Cindy. Jeez, remember my heart, honey.' You let the blow melt into a hug. She is dirty and sweaty and shaking and just about the most awesome thing you have ever held in your arms.

Mike says, deadpan, 'Jeez, Mike. Thank heavens you're OK too.'

Cindy disentangles herself from your arms. You become aware Mike is looking at you strangely. 'Don't hold your breath, kid. I don't hug guys.'

His expression gets a little stranger then. He is looking behind you. You turn. The new toy is looming over the crate you are using for cover.

It's seven feet of natural-born killer and it's looking straight at you.

– 3 –

A cow saves your life.

With timing slicker than a card shark it wanders between you and the new toy. The toy recognises it as a non-target and gets confused. For a moment it stands there trying to work out how three legitimate human targets can suddenly turn into one non-threatening, non-legitimate-target bovine ruminant. For a moment you feel sorry for it; the thing is as smart as a five-card flush but it lacks imagination crucial to efficient operation.

Of course if the damn thing had fired anyway the cow would have been vapor along with all

202

three of you. Fortunately for you the toy's speed of thought is as fast as the Cap'n thought. It stops itself firing with several hundred milliseconds to spare.

It turns to seek new targets. Its confusion fades as targets present themselves. You hear screams, the sizzle of burning flesh and the bell-like ringing of falling metallic objects.

You grab Mike and Cindy and drag them away crouched low to the ground, making damn sure to keep the cow between you and sudden, gut-vaporising death.

'Where we going?'

'Yeah. We'll never escape from that thing.'

'Not while we're on the *Regalia* anyway.'

You sigh impatiently. How can two such depressingly perfect physical specimens of humanity be gifted with such empty cargo pods for brains? 'That's why we're leaving the *Regalia*.'

'We are?'

'Sure we are – if I can just figure out how to steer this damn cow.'

You manage this by the simple expedient of kicking the animal in the direction you want it to go. After a few false starts you manage to get it headed in the right direction.

You get all the way to the cargo deck control room in this manner.

Two jackers are manning the room; you can

hear them making up excuses not to go and help in the fight.

'Better stay here and man the operations systems.'

'Right.'

'Could be disastrous if not.'

'I'm with ya.'

'Anyone could operate the systems if we weren't here.'

'Right.'

'Then where would we be?'

'With ya.'

'Spaced, that's where: if the Cap'n ever found out.'

'I heard he was dead.'

'The Cap'n?'

'Right.'

'You heard that?'

'Yep.'

'Better stay here and man the operations systems then.'

'Right.'

You edge the cow closer. You need to get a look-see at the control panel. The quick glance you get is enough to show you your plan – apparently suicidal though it is – stands a depressingly good chance of success.

You become aware the cow has gained unwanted attention.

'Here, Harry.'

'Yeah?'

'Is that a cow?'

You fire off a few shots near the cow and it does exactly what you hoped it would: it runs in a blind panic straight into the control room.

In the ensuing confusion you jump into the room, slap both hands down on the control marked:

CARGO BAY DOORS:
EMERGENCY DEPRESSURISATION

Between the three of you and the cow the two jackers are hopelessly outgunned. One jacker fires on the cow. He realises this is a stupid thing to do only after the animal falls on him, breaking both his legs and his right hip. Cindy smashes the other on the head with a gun when he bends to help the first.

You grab Mike and Cindy, drag them out of the room.

About half a mile away there is a rumbling sound like distant thunder as the cargo deck doors begin to open. In keeping with the storm motif, the air is already swirling in knots and eddies, picking up loose trash and scooting it towards the big empty.

'What the hell have you done? We'll suffocate!'

'Quit panicking, Mike. There's probably seventeen cubic miles of air in here. It'll take ages to leak into space. Long enough for us to get to *Betty* anyway.'

As if to prove you wrong the wind gets up – and shoves a gout of flame from an exploding cargo pod towards you. Cindy swears loudly and dives back into the control room. You follow her and slam the door.

The flame belches past, the windows implode and you are pelted with glass shrapnel and scorched air.

You smell cooking cow.

Then the control panel explodes. Gravity fades away as the cargo deck quits rotating.

Mike stares at the smoking remains of the control panel. 'You better hope these guys have a backup system.'

'You mean to tell me you never heard of the Titanic?'

'The what?'

'Never mind. I'll tell you later in the lifeboats.'

Then you're out of the control room and running, and the very elements are trying to take you down. The cargo deck is like a ship in a storm. Everything is loose now. Tools, jackers, pods, cargo, machinery, trailers, cranes, clothing – everything is being whipped into a frenzy by the rush of air and whirled towards the still opening cargo bay doors.

A string of explosions ripple nearby as one of the jacked rigs goes up trailer by trailer until the cab itself explodes. Flame and smoke join the storm of loose trash. Wind whips the fire-damping foam into sticky rain. Somewhere an emergency siren is hooting like a mad giant's laughter.

Jackers yell uselessly at each other. The new toy stalks through the chaos, unaffected by the confusion, methodically hunting down and killing anything that isn't a cow.

Dodging the lethal trash you try to pull yourself towards *Betty*. It's no good. She's off to spinward and the doors are dead ahead now. The wind is carrying you straight towards them – and the stars you can see glimmering in the big dark beyond.

Fighting for breath you clutch at the nearest piece of metal to slow your speed. It's the arm of a loading crane.

You get an idea.

You grab the others and swing aboard. You pray like mad there's enough juice in the jets to get you to *Betty*.

There is – just.

But as you approach *Betty* a new problem presents itself. The new toy is waiting for you beside the rig. It tilts its head to target you as the crane swings closer.

'Jeez – we're dead!'

Without bothering to tell Mike to shut up you aim the crane at the toy and wedge the accelerator pedal to the floor. Grabbing Cindy and Mike you jump off the crane seconds before it slams into the toy and explodes.

The last you see of it, the toy is tumbling backwards, limbs akimbo, various pieces of scorched jacker impaled on extended blades, plasma bolts frying every last surface in sight.

You pull yourself towards the rig – but the air flow has started *Betty* tumbling towards the cargo bay doors, trailers in tow, skidding and sparking across the deck. 'How the hell are we gonna get aboard?'

'Shut up and jump. It's our only chance.'

You know if you wait you're a dead man, so you jump on instinct. *Betty* knows you're coming. She won't kill you.

You hope.

You grab a thruster cowling, pull yourself round to the airlock. Mike and Cindy are close behind. The rig is tilting over for another shot at the deck.

You manage to scramble into the airlock roughly a second before the deck slams against the coaming. You slap the button to cycle the airlock shut.

Nothing happens. You slap it again and again. Nothing. No movement of the hatch, no clean, cool metal bulkhead to seal you off from the incipient decompression.

You swear, kick the control panel – and remember that Ass-face blew the hatch open when you were captured.

You scramble through the lock and into the 'pit.

'Get the suits on – fast!'

Air is whistling out of the rig to join the storm of trash hurling itself into the big dark. There are no lights in the rig since the jackers powered her down to conserve the batteries they were planning to steal.

Getting the suits on is a nightmare.

With the job half done you boot up the nav-systems. The five-hour cooldown has worked wonders for the autobutler. The systems are online and grinning about it. You tell *Betty* to get the hell out of here. She doesn't need any second urging. She scurries free of the cargo bay amidst a billow of trash, dead jackers, smashed machinery and ruptured cows.

One glance in the rearview is enough to tell you your troubles aren't over yet. The *Regalia* has begun a slow tumble. In a ship twelve miles long this is a fast ride to suicide. She breaks apart in the midsection as you watch. Back broken, she hangs before the stars for a moment before the reactors lose it. Then she's a white hot cloud of gas puffing out through a lethal mess of shattered metal, black rock and asteroids.

Betty scoots away fast. Well, she's still damaged, so she kind of skids sideways away from the cloud of lethal scrap that was the *Regalia*, avoiding the worst of the blast by placing the trailers between herself and the explosion.

You sigh. 'Some days I wonder why the hell I got outta bed.'

Nobody answers, for which you are grateful.

Then you catch sight of the trailers in the rearview and realise you still have a problem.

In fact you have an army of problems.

Every one of them stuck more firmly to your ass than piles.

Intercourse

– 1 –

It takes you three hours to fix the airlock. By then the air in the suits is gone and you are working on O-two from the emergency supply tucked away in the escape pod. You haven't been able to tie on to the main supply; the recharge tap is located in the airlock and was damaged beyond repair when the jackers boarded. Finally the leak is repaired. You flood the 'pit with O-two, check for leaks and then try to catch a little shut-eye.

Some time later you wake with your normal raging headache and even more normal bad temper. Someone's banging on something. Loud. Annoyingly loud. You slide out of your bed, look around for the culprit. The rig's a mess, your Gibson twelve-string is totalled, the Flytrap is dead, the board missing several darts lost in the outrush of air; now someone's banging on the wall, apparently just to ruin your beauty sleep.

Either Mike or Cindy is going to get a mighty large piece of your mind.

Except they're still tucked up in their beds asleep.

You look around the 'pit. Nothing's of any help. Even the mustard stains on the nearest screen stubbornly refuse to form into any mystical patterns of information. Whoever is banging is not in the rig. The sound isn't coming from the walls or the kitchen. After a moment you realise it's coming from the hatch leading to the cargo crawlway. From the *other side* of the hatch. The side leading to the cargo trailers.

You wake Mike and Cindy. You give Cindy the blaster you swiped from a dying jacker, then you and Mike suit up.

'Are you sure this is such a good idea? What if it's more of those warrior things?'

'Honey, if it was they'd have bust their way in here and fried us by now.'

'You sure about that?'

You shake your head curtly. 'Nope. But someone's gotta check that noise out.'

You begin to pull your suit back on. It's little enough protection against the Cap'n's toys and you all know it. Cindy gives you a concerned look.

'It's OK. I'll be careful.'

'Promise me.'

'I promise. Mike, you comin' along? If the shit hits the fan I could use another pair of hands to help with the shovelin'.'

Mike shrugs and suits up as well. You tell

Betty to open the crawlway hatch. You grip your blaster, crouch down and step through into the crawlspace beyond.

The crawlway is empty except for a bundle of blood-stained rags.

You step closer. The rags move. Metal gleams. Mike aims his blaster. You place a hand on his shoulder. He holds fire. The metal gleams again. Something bangs.

The bundle of rags moves again, jerks, turns to face you. Somehow you aren't surprised.

It's Cap'n Macanudo.

It's half of him, anyway.

From the waist up he's a mess. Blood, melted glass and armour. Human arm gone from the elbow. Devil's eye wide and staring, the lens cracked, aqueous humour leaking along his ravaged cheek like tears.

From the waist down he is gone. A fused mess of metal and flesh where his waist had been is all that is keeping him alive.

Using his demon's arm he flips himself over. He reaches for a breast pocket. Once again Mike lifts the gun. Once again you stop him firing.

The Cap'n takes a cigar from his pocket and jams it into his blood-encrusted mouth.

'Light me.'

Thankful for the helmet which prevents the stench from reaching your nostrils, you reach into the pocket the Cap'n indicates. You pull out a lighter, click it open. The Cap'n flinches away from the light of the flame. He shudders. A look of terror flits across his face. You imagine the last thing he must have seen: the bright glare of the killing beam from his new toy as it bisected his body. Wincing in sympathy, you close the lighter. He shakes his head. Crisped flesh crackles. 'Canyon. Light me.'

You click open the lighter again. A moment later the Cap'n is puffing weakly on his cigar. The smile he gives as he tastes the smoke almost makes you cry.

Mike pushes up his helmet visor. 'I'll . . . get the first aid kit.'

The cigar waves impatiently. 'Forget it. The major arteries are cauterised. But I won't be playing the drums again.'

You push up your own visor, gasp momentarily at the stench of burning flesh. 'What happened back there on the *Regalia*?'

The Cap'n sucks on his cigar, coughs blood. He touches the blood on his chin, looks at his metal fingertips, then gestures with the cigar. 'These things'll kill you.' He has another coughing fit. He manages a nod in the direction of the hatch leading back into the cargo trailers. 'Soldiers. Warriors. My new toys. Two of them activated. They do that in geometric waves. One.

214

Two. Four. Eight. You know the math. Then they did what they're programmed by E.J. Saggs to do. They sought out the imperfect, the low lifes and losers, the impoverished, the dying . . . and they removed their genes from the genepool.'

'They killed them, you mean?'

'They killed them.'

You don't need to think too hard about the Cap'n's words. 'That's what's in the trailers isn't it? An army.'

The Cap'n manages a nod. 'A biomechanical army.'

'Bio-what?' Mike hasn't got it yet. 'You mean like in those movies?'

You let the Cap'n explain. 'Yes son, like the movies. Only nastier. The toys are a mix of biological life systems and mechanical components. Strength and intelligence. The ultimate warrior. I made 'em for the Company. So Saggs could take over the Earth Government.'

'By fighting the Earth military?'

A coughing fit, then. 'No. Earth is a hive of sickness and poverty. Saggs planned to use the toys to start a war. Then he'd use things like these –' the Cap'n waves his remote deactivator weakly in your face '– to deactivate the warriors. He'd have removed an undesirable portion of the genepool and at the same time been so popular with the masses that he would have had no trouble being voted into office as President.'

You want to be sick. It isn't just the smell.

'How can we stop him?'

The Cap'n smiles. His lip splits, releasing a fresh flow of blood. 'You're carrying his army. Stop the army and you stop the man.'

You shrug. 'So we don't go to Earth.'

The Cap'n grins again. 'Checked your course lately? These trailers ain't just fitted with smart-guns, you know.'

'Meaning?'

'The toys are designed to carry out their pro-gramming at any cost. To carry out their pro-gramming they have to reach Earth.'

Mike looks puzzled.

You explain it to him. 'He means whatever damn computer is running the trailer guns has probably jacked into *Betty*'s navicomp. Short of destroying the rig there's no way we can avoid going to Earth.'

The Cap'n wheezes. You realise he's agreeing with you.

You take the remote device from his hand, tak-ing care to make sure your fingers don't come within the ambit of his metal ones. 'You gonna tell me how to work this gizmo?'

He shrugs. Well, insofar as you can shrug with one mechanical arm and one arm missing from the elbow down. 'Sure. Two buttons. Green for go. Red for stop. Same as traffic lights.' A laugh turns into a gurgling cough. His breathing jerks, stalls. He manages to hold out his cigar. 'Say, you want to . . . finish this? It's really . . . rather . . . good.' The last word comes out as a wet rattle.

He doesn't live to hear your answer.

It's just as well; you hate cigars.

– 2 –

Then the whole trailer hatch burns through in a blaze of melting metal and the whole cigar thing is academic anyway.

Air gushes out of the crawlway into the already decompressed trailer. What remains of the Cap'n begins to ooze out of his metallic frame.

Two of the new toys step through the melted gap, pushing aside the softened metal as if it were cardboard. The gap behind is filled with the dark shapes of two more.

Mike raises his gun.

You place a hand on his arm. He holds fire.

The toys stare at him. They think about you.

'What's the deal?'

'Shhh!'

The toys move forward. In step, like toy soldiers – only they're patently not toys. They move like dancers. Fast but steady, completely in control.

217

They continue towards you. Mike looks like he's about to get in their way. He raises his blaster. The leading toy tracks the movement. You grab the gun, throw it and your own to one side. They tumble down the crawlway and bounce off the far wall. The toy tracks them effortlessly, head turning a full one-eighty faster than a skidding joy-rider.

A glare and the guns are vapor. So is half the crawlway wall. The rest of the air vanishes from the crawlway. The toys resume their advance towards the 'pit.

You pull Mike out of their way.

They draw level. Lenses swivel to watch you. Or target you. They step past. Four sets of clawed metallic feet moving in perfect silence, making not even the smallest vibration to run through the decking and into your suit.

The first pair draws level.

You remain absolutely still.

They move past. The second pair draws level. One brushes your elbow.

It turns. Looks at you.

It's too much for Mike. He is off, pulling himself towards the 'pit, shouting a warning to Cindy over the comm.

The toys target him.

You raise the Cap'n's deactivator. It works like a charm. In less than a second the deadly killers

218

are nothing more than post-modernist black
metal sculptures, frozen into positions of comic
menace.

Mike turns. He sees what you have done. 'Jeez,
Canyon. Your timing is pretty scary.'

You don't bother to answer. Instead you pull
yourself over to the nearest toy and examine it.
You reach out a gloved hand to touch the shell.
The glove slips over the surface as if it were made
of ice. No friction. Now the toy is stationary you
can see its outline more clearly. Its shell is black,
not smooth but studded with fine antennae-like
hairs. Radar? Sonar? Air pressure detectors? Its
skull and back and chest are covered with them.

Mike touches the wire-like hairs. 'Do you suppose it can see all around?'

'Dunno if "see" is the right word exactly, but
yeah, wouldn't surprise me. I mean, what could
be more useful to a soldier than to be able to see
over your shoulder without turning your head?'

Mike nods. 'Check out these arms.' He points
to the upper limbs. A long slot splits the outside
of the arm casing. Within, light gleams from the
edge of a curved blade. The blade extends from
the wrist, doubling the arm length.

You remember the warrior on the *Regalia*,
how it impaled a jacker standing three feet
behind it without even looking around.

You begin to examine the rest of the toy, but

Mike's had enough. 'Man, I've had it. Let's get the hell outta here.'

You shake your head. 'You ask yourself what they were doing yet? Why they didn't attack us?'

Obviously he hasn't. 'Well, we didn't attack them – guess they thought we weren't a threat.'

'I reckon it's simpler than that. I think we were just outside their programming.'

'What do you mean?'

'They were heading for the 'pit. Think about what the Cap'n said before he died. "Checked your course lately?" That's what he said. I bet the damn trailer's jacked into the navicomp – and those things were revived to make sure we were on course.'

'Jeez.' You see his brain starting to work. 'Cindy –'

'She'll be fine.'

'But –'

'Mike, she'll be fine.'

'Shouldn't we at least try to change course?'

'And let them know we're on to them? Then we would be a threat, right? And you know what that would mean. Anyway it's an hour yet till we make orbit. I think we ought to take another look at these trailers. See if the Cap'n's little charm will put the rest of his babies to sleep before they wake up.'

'This is a bad idea.'

'Some days, kid, just waking up is a bad idea. Come on.'

– 3 –

The trailer is just as you remember it – a mess of tubes and organ sacs, a junkyard of neatly stacked metallic implants and limbs. The hole the jackers blew in the side is still open. Stars glimmer faintly through the spaces between the tubes and sacs.

There are six empty spaces with limp, dripping tubes to signify the six toys which have already awakened, two on the *Regalia*, four here on *Betty*.

The rest are asleep, folded neatly into spiky packages, attached to the tubes which provide their life support.

Nothing moves.

Yet.

You aim the Cap'n's charm at the nearest coiled bundle of organics and metallics. You push the red button.

Nothing happens.

Then again, if it had worked, nothing would happen, would it?

Something moves. A hint of something uncoiling glimpsed out of the corner of your eye – then all hell breaks loose with terrifying speed.

Tubes unknot, fluids boil, sacs expand and

221

contract. Some of the metal junk shuffles into place to enclose organics. Limbs unfurl and harden, the skull expands and trifurcates, lenses blink wetly, fingers clench in life-spasm. The whole thing is a self-building three-dimensional jigsaw from hell and it's coming to life as you watch.

You reach for Mike but he needs no second urging. He's already on the way out. You join him, toys unravelling into life behind you, one for every step you take.

Two in the *Regalia*. Four here on *Betty*.

Eight this time.

'I thought the damn thing was supposed to shut them down not wake them up!'

You frown as you run. 'Me too. Maybe they perceived the shutdown command as an attack.'

'Great! Now we're all hogmeat!'

Another two steps and there is more than the suggestion of movement behind you. The tubes sway like forest creepers in a heavy wind as you force a way through. The movement from behind spreads to either side. Two of the newly awakened toys block your exit into the crawlway.

You shut them down with the charm and keep running.

Immediately sixteen more sets of organics uncoil and begin to lace themselves into protective armour.

'Shit! Every time we shut one down it starts the cycle over again.'

'How many awake now?'

'How the hell do I know? I never could sprint and do math at the same time.'

Mike works it out. 'We had eight, you shut down two, sixteen more woke up. Twenty-two? Yeah. Twenty-two. Jesus fuck a shit souffle – we really are hogmeat, Canyon!'

'Ever the optimist, right Mike?'

Another toy steps out of the coiling tubes. The lenses track you but do not fire. They can't shoot you without damaging the trailer interior. You back away. The arm blades unfold, swinging out and locking into position easily. Now you're back in arm's reach again. The arms move, ergonomic stabbing movements, avoiding the tubes and organics with depressing ease.

'Mike – split up. And be careful. One tear in your suit and that's all she wrote.'

Mike takes the hint, vanishes into the jungle of writhing tubes.

You catch a glimpse of at least six of the toys making for the breach in the hull. More are moving purposefully towards the crawlway.

Firing the Cap'n's charm as you move, you swing through the coiling tubes towards the crawlway. Toys freeze all around you. You

223

move, humming Emmylou Harris. It's musical statues and you're *it*.

You freeze two toys who are a hand's breadth from impaling Mike in four different places, then pull yourself towards the crawlway.

Eight more are in there. You spray them with infra-red sleepy-bye commands and they nod off obediently.

Mike catches you up and says breathlessly, 'Cindy –'

'Right there with you.'

You force a way through the stationary monsters, unclipping an arm blade as you go. As a sword it is hard to hold and heavy, but it's better than nothing.

Mike grabs a sword too; he tests it on a warrior. The blade cuts alloy and organics with equal ease, shearing a limb and leaving the stump leaking blood and marrow into the vacuum.

He heads for the 'pit, one thought in his mind. You hesitate. Then with one angry blow you sever the head of the nearest toy. You grab it, lenses, power pack and all, and head for the 'pit in Mike's wake. You wave the head and screech as you pull yourself along. You're so charged with adrenalin you don't even know it's you screaming.

Behind you thirty-two toys are waking up. Beyond them the sliding hatch to trailer number two is hinging open and in the dark space beyond lights are beginning to glimmer.

You join Mike and Cindy in the 'pit. You fill Cindy in on the gory details as you rig a jumplead from the toy's head to *Betty*'s portable systems-fault locator. Trying to use the toy's weapon against them is not much of a chance – but it's the only damn chance you've got.

Cindy scrambles into a suit and then helps Mike use a patch welder to seal the crawlway hatch. Not that it'll make the slightest bit of difference when the toys come calling. Good for morale though.

You glance up as the hull gongs.

Footsteps. The toys are on the hull.

The hatch begins to glow.

Mike hands one of the arm blades to Cindy. She wields it with the same defiance she wielded your Gibson twelve-string when the jackers blew the lock.

Mike glances your way. 'What the hell you playing with that ball of crap for, John?'

'This ball of crap's our ticket to glory, kid.' You throw him the Cap'n's charm. 'Now buy me some time, right?'

Mike nods.

You grab another handful of leads, plug them in.

The hatch grows hotter.

Footsteps ring on the hull.

'How you comin' with the gizmo, John?'

'Old fingers make slow work, kid. Now shut up and let me work.'

The hatch begins to dissolve. Sparks fly.

You scramble with the last connections and boot up the portable.

Metal runs like taffy. Mike and Cindy back away from the heat.

'John. I don't want to rush you man, but we're up against it here.' Mike's voice is breaking with tension. Cindy says nothing, just braces her feet and grips the blade a little tighter.

'I hear you.'

You begin typing commands into the portable.

Nothing. The lenses remain dark.

Footsteps ring on the hull, again and again.

You thump the portable.

Nothing.

Hatch metal drips in lazy globules into the 'pit.

You type in more commands. More. Nothing.

The crawlway hatch melts through. Toys shoulder aside the flaking metal and step into the 'pit.

The windscreen shatters and more toys step over the dashboard.

Blades unfold.

Lenses blink.

'Kid!'

Mike waves the Cap'n's charm around the 'pit, one sweeping gesture that encompasses every toy in sight. 'Suck on this popsicle, assholes!'

Nothing happens. The toys don't stop.

Mike hits the button again. And again.

Claws rattle. Grasping metal fingers unfold.

Mike thumps it against his helmet and tries again. Nothing. A red light blinks. 'Goddamn tight-fisted, steel-anused bastard fitted his charm with cheap batteries!'

'John – we're outta juice here.'

'We're fucked!'

There's more movement then – both Mike and Cindy swinging their blades like insane Norse gods; glittering arcs whose offensive properties are, for the moment, beyond the toys' experience. Limbs sever. Organic mush bursts free in gluey strings. Some of it sizzles against the molten hatch metal. They keep fighting. You grit your teeth. They're dead and don't know it.

You thump the portable. Nothing.

A toy moves closer and –

– you kick the skull and –

– the blades unfold and –

– butt the skull and –

– *the lenses blink open.*

'Jesus H. goddamn Christ in his great steel wheels, people, we are cooking!'

It's time to kick some biomechanical ass.

227

You raise the skull and fry the nearest toy. The blast goes on to take out the navicomp and three metres of hull immediately behind it.

You throttle down to a fine beam, sweep the 'pit.

Toys puff into vapour in eerie silence.

Blades swing.

Limbs thrash and float away.

Mike lops the legs off a toy and pushes it back out the windscreen. It vanishes into the big dark. Cindy hacks off another toy's head in customary silence.

You're hip deep in organic mush and machine parts by now. Chunks of flesh and metal scrap drift around in ever-thickening banks. It's getting hard to see.

More toys come in. You melt them to slag.

All you can hear is heavy breathing. Mike and Cindy. All you can feel is the occasional thud as some severed bit of toy gongs against the hull.

That and your heartbeat, hammering at your ribcage.

That and the blood pounding in your ears.

That and the killing rage screaming in your head and heart and veins as you wield the severed skull and its killing beam like a sword made out of the very light of hell itself.

Then something else.

A gasp, a quivering pain in your chest and you're
too old for this shit, too old by half and you're
screaming as your arm goes dead and you're
heart is old just
screaming in defiance and you're
too damn old and
screaming at Cindy, screaming it's OK, it's OK for her to love Mike because
now you're gonna pay the price and
you fall and
you forgive them and
you feel blades slash at your suit and tug holes in it and air is gushing out of your lungs and your grip on the skull is gone and your grip on life is nearly gone and the blades are cutting, cutting, opening your suit and opening your heart and

– 5 –

suddenly everything screams back into focus with absolute clarity. You try to speak. What comes out is a hacking stutter, a gasp for breath and a shuddering scream.

When you finally open your eyes you see the last toy with its blades a heartbeat from your suit. Aunt Hettie's microwave oven is smashed down on to its head. Goop seeps out from underneath in sticky strings.

Mike and Cindy are staring at you and making

goldfish movements with their mouths.

After an eternity you realise they are yelling with delight.

They are yelling your name.

Mike is holding a heart syringe labelled: *adrenalin*.

– 6 –

Betty slips effortlessly into high Earth orbit. It's a miracle considering the damage she has sustained.

You tell Mike and Cindy they have to take the escape pod.

They argue.

Bloody kids.

You struggle into a sitting position and tell them why.

'We still got half a mile of trailers behind us that ain't planning on letting go until they hit dirt. Well, I'm gonna show them hitting dirt is no fun.'

'You're gonna crash *Betty*?' Cindy's eyes are wide. 'But you'll –'

You manage a grin. 'Not me, honey. I'll swing her around, use the trailers for a heat shield. I done it before.'

'That was on Mars – a sixth of the gravity –'

'Got no choice.'

'John, the Pachyderm 2000 wasn't built to –'

'Goddamn it all to hell, kid, I'm sick of hearing you whine about what the Pachyderms can or cannot do. Now this is what's what. You take the pod. I'll junk the trailers. I'll ride *Bitchin' Betty* in on a tail of flame a mile high and meet you at the Church of First Exit Off The Freeway to give Cindy away at the wedding.'

They're still arguing as you push them into the pod.

'There's room in here. We can scrunch up –'

'I told you before. There's room for two –' you reach for something, jam it through the hatch '– and my lucky dartboard. If I don't make it, you play a game for me, you hear? And you remember John Canyon and *Bitchin' Betty*. You hear me now? You hear?'

Their reply is lost as the hatch slams shut.

The pod blasts clear with a crushing jerk.

– 7 –

You try to boot up the navicomp. Nothing cooking. *Betty*'s CPU is dead as old hogs, taken out in the firefight with the Cap'n's toys. You might even have done it yourself, with the same blast with which you fried that first warrior.

You feel tears sting your eyes.

You grip the stick in both hands, jam your feet on the pedals.

You wipe mustard from the afterburner panel,

program the attitude jets manually. The 'pit shakes as *Betty* turns ass downwards to the atmosphere. The Earth swings out of view and is replaced by the Moon, shining half full, square on in the shattered windscreen.

You take a better grip on the stick. '*Betty*. I know your CPU's shot an' all but I got something to say and now's the time.' You try to wipe away a tear but your gloved hand hits the visor and skids away. '*Betty*. We been a long time together, you and I. Fifteen years. Like an old married couple. I treated you right, didn't I? Hell, I know I swore at you that time on Oberon when the coupling linkage bust but you know I didn't mean it. And I guess I kicked your primary manifold more times'n I like to recall. And . . . I know things ain't been so peachy between us of late. Hell, the long and the short of it is this: I thought Cindy was the gal for me. I was wrong. It's you, *Betty*. It's always been you. Till death us do part, baby.'

Earth is swelling in the rearview, a glorious ball of blue-white fluff, the pot of gold at the end of hell's rainbow.

You whisper a last apology to *Betty* and drop her into the atmosphere.

Turbulence slaps you round the ass.

The trailers cook, melt, erupt into charred garbage which peels off in a smoky contrail.

Betty shakes, a dying spasm. Old rig. Old

232

heart. No adrenalin left. Flame edges the open cockpit. More flame edges your vision.

The toys scream and burn. Wriggling stick-figures flicker past in a blur of molten metal.

One grabs the wreckage of the windscreen coaming and begins to climb in. It reaches for you, arms, legs, chest unravelling into strings of molten metal as it comes.

You grin, though you've no idea why. You laugh because it's better than crying.

Molten fingers reach for your helmet.

It doesn't matter.

Old rig. Old heart.

Only one thing left to do.

You give the dying toy the finger, slam the pedal to the metal and ride *Bitchin' Betty* in on a tail of flame a mile high.

Till death us do part.

Undeniable

– 1 –

Heaven is sterile and full of doctors.

The music of the spheres is Emmylou Harris piped in on local FM.

The angel looking at you is Cindy's mother.

– 2 –

Eternity is eighteen days in Palmdale Spaceport Medical Center.

– 3 –

Mike and Cindy are there when you wake up for the hundred-and-whatever time.

In eager gulps they tell you about it.

The trailers are gone. The toys are dead. You ejected at low altitude and parachuted to safety seconds before *Betty* burnt up. You had a heart attack on landing. Another one. You sailed through it. Well, maybe not sailed exactly, but you survived.

You stare at the wedding band on Cindy's finger as they prattle on.

After a while she notices. 'We wanted to wait

234

. . . I wanted you to give me away . . . we didn't know if you were gonna . . . you know . . .' She stops. She starts to cry. It's the first time you've ever seen her cry.

She covers her face and leaves the room. Mike goes with her.

The angel comes back. 'So you're John Canyon. I heard all about you. I'm Carol. Cindy's mother.'

She tells you all about her operation. She was in stasis. They defrosted her. They cured her. She's whole and well and young and beautiful, with the same Brooklyn drawl as her daughter, and suddenly all you can think about is getting up off the bed and ditching the intravenous lines and dancing a square jig to local FM.

She becomes aware that you are staring.

You don't care. Blame the medication.

The fact is Cindy's mother is young enough to be your –

No. She's not. She's old enough to be your –

No. She's not. She's –

She's grinning at your confusion.

You don't care. Blame the medication.

Her smile is as bright as the moon, as wide as forever.

'John Canyon, I heard you was dead. I hope for the sake of my sex life you ain't.'

4

E.J. Saggs comes to visit you with a news team while you're convalescing. Seems he's bought the Presidency when the Government was privatised and didn't need the damn toys anyhow.

Now he wants to buy you off with a suitcase full of cash – more cash than you've hauled loads. Enough cash to set you and half a dozen friends up for life.

Problem is, Carol doesn't want you to take it.

Cindy doesn't want you to take it.

Mike doesn't want you to take it.

Hell, you don't really want to take it yourself.

You take the cash, make promises of silence and allegiance you have no intention of keeping. E.J. Saggs goes away happy.

But then something about the smarmy fat fucker's grateful smile makes you want to puke. You get to thinking of *Betty* frying up there in orbit for no reason at all and how much you're going to miss her and how much you've lost.

You throw the suitcase out of the window in a fit of anger.

The bomb hidden inside it explodes square on top of E.J. Saggs' limousine. It rains burning cash for half an hour. The press have a field day.

5

They elect a new president and he gives you a

new rig. A Mammoth 3000. She ain't as cute as *Betty* but she's big enough for a family of four and works like a horse. You call her *Bitchin' Betty Too*.

You and Carol and Cindy and Mike take her out for a little spin. She's a fine rig, with many a year of cargo hauling in her. She's so fine you begin to get the glimmerings of an idea. You park *Betty* in high Earth orbit. With the Moon shining above you let them have it right between the eyes.

'Carol, I say the hell with independents. Let's get married, form a company of our own, earn shitloads of money, raise a posse of kids and live happily ever after. That goes for you too, Mike and Cindy. A four-way split, evens up, on every load we haul.

'Ladies and gentlemen, that's the deal on the table. Whaddaya say?'

Acknowledgements: biting the bullet

In the words of John Canyon, 'In this business, respect is as rare as rocking-horse shit.' There's a lot of truth in those words. So in order to provide a balance I would like to respectfully dedicate this novel to all the people that made it possible; all the people that made it good. And to anyone, anywhere who has the self-respect to do the best job they can no matter how crap the money is and how late the cheque arrives.

And those people are:

Paul Hinder	(the Professor Pat. Pending of the editing keys)
Rob Kirby	(for bruising bottoms that needed bruising)
Trees	(for saying 'Yes')
Giz	(for being fluffy and disgusting above and beyond the call of nature)
Thomas	(currently fighting on the side of the Vorlons in the First Great Shadow War)

Obviously I would also like to say hi to the family and folks at home. Mum, Mindy, Brandy, Jop, Jo, Steve, Andrea, Lynne, Lizzie, Huw, Jo, Tim, Kurt, Andy and Helen, Andy and Sue, Alan and Alis, Owen and Jackie, Steve and Belinda, Lee, Nacula, Lalitha, Simon, Nige and Debs, Debs and Penny, Sam, Nick, Benjamin, Daniel and all the little fluffy wonders, especially Stumpy.

In case I never get to write another *Babylon* novel, I would like to take this opportunity to thank all those who were able to give such positive comments on Clarke's Law over the Internet. I would also like to thank those that gave negative comments. Hell, guys, at least you got off your asses and did something, right?

A special mention, in case I don't get another opportunity, to Tom Bateman (thanks for the *B5* idea) and Psicorps. (Don't worry, Darren, your days are numbered . . . promise!)

An extra special mention for Huw's mum and dad (helpful tips on cleaning the bathroom no. 1: chuck in a hand grenade, shut the door and run like hell . . .)

This novel, among others, is dedicated to my father, Colin Booth Mortimore, who died earlier this year. He took no bullshit and he gave no bullshit. I think he'd have liked John Canyon.